MINT JULEP

By

MARTHA JAMES

Illustrated by

REGINALD F. BOLLES

NEW YORK

W. D. LANE & CO.

1909

CONTENTS

CONTENTS

LIST OF ILLUSTRATIONS

MINT JULEP
A NEW ENGLAND STORY

MINT JULEP
A NEW ENGLAND STORY

CHAPTER I

TOM JULEP, farmer of Little Acres, struck a match and proceeded to light a small lamp on the kitchen table, while his sturdy son, who had just returned from Boston, where he had gone in the early Spring to work for a large Ice Company, drew a chair and seated himself before the stove.

Although it was nearly five months since he had been inside the little farm house that was "home," he evinced no interest.

"Yer mother's gone ter bed," said the older man, drawing up a chair opposite that of his son. "Yer see we didn't ex-

1

pect yer, and the train was late; did yer
know why it was late?"

There was something more than a de-
sire to gratify mere curiosity in that question; Tom wanted to get his son started
talking in the hope of hearing something
of the outside world, of the great bustling
city that he had just left behind.

The old man had been to Boston once
some twenty years ago, and memories of
that eventful occasion were still fresh in
his mind and made him long to hear about
the big city, what was going on there,
and all the wonderful experiences that
his son must have had in five long months.

But it was no easy task to get this
young man to talk.

Not that Tom expected him to say much
even then, for William Julep had never
been known to say anything unless it was
imperatively necessary, and when he did,
the words seemed to cling like the leaves
on a winter's oak.

"Did yer know that the train was late,
William?"

"Ya'as I thought 'twas late, father."

"Yes 'twas; ef you'd let us know you was comin' I'd a been there to meet yer, but yer not much hand ter write, William."

After a few minutes in which the old man saw that no answer was forthcoming, he thought he would make another venture.

"How did yer like the ice business?"

"Fust rate."

"Glad ter hear it," and Tom, surprised at the prompt answer, looked keenly at his son, half hoping for a bit of news to follow, but after waiting a reasonable length of time, when it did not come, he ventured once again into the barren waste of William's conversational powers.

"I expect Boston's a wonderful taown now, a pretty live place, take it all in all, eh William?"

"Ya'as 'tis, father."

"Suppose you'll try it again?"

"Hard ter tell."

In the long silence that followed, the

clock on the little shelf above them made so much noise that a cat, dozing behind the stove, opened one eye, only to close it gently again and stretch out her black paws in drowsy content.

When five fruitless minutes had ticked away, Tom gave a long audible yawn and stretching both arms over his head slowly arose from the chair.

"Wa'al son, guess I'll be off ter bed."

At this remark William cleared his throat and glanced at his father as if meditating speech. Tom saw the movement, and so fearful was he of breaking the spell that he let his arms remain suspended for a moment and then settled back in his chair.

"Anything special doin' while yer was in Boston, William?" he asked by way of encouragement.

"I was jest a'goin' ter ask yer what's yer idee of marriage, father?"

"Marriage" echoed Tom, gazing steadfastly at his son.

"Wa'al William, marriage is the nat-

ural condition o' man, an', like some other
natural conditions, ye've got ter make the
best of it. A man could be happy 'thout
a wife, but he don't allus know it till he's
hed one; not that I'm agin matrimony,
far from it; take it all in all, it's the greatest institootion on this planet.

"But look a here son, why do they go
outer ther way ter assure us that in
Heaven there's no marriage nor givin' in
marriage? I'm not sayin' that is held out
as a injuicement, not at all, but it sets
enybody thinkin' a whole lot.

"It's jest like this, William, a man gits
married; he endows a female with all his
worldly goods if he happens to have any,
and hisself thrown in. Naow he has most
o' her human nater and all his own. *She*
don't count on that. An' she has some
o' his human nater, besides a brand pe-
culiar to her sex; *he* don't count on that.
Fact is they haven't reckoned c'rect, and
the fust thing yer know, they run right
inter a squall.

"Naow if he happens to be the right

kind o' captain, and she a fair mate,
they'll git inter clear water agin, and look
out fer squalls in the future; — if not,
they'll keep on, strike a hurricane some
day an' go ter pieces in ther dervorce
court. William, the ways o' wimmen
is allus open ter specalation — they're
doubtful critters, the best o' them, on-
sartin at times as a stray hen, but tell
'em they're right nine times outer ten, an'
the tenth time jest remark casally they're
not wrong, then you go ahead an' do
what you think c'rect. If a man follers
that course, marriage won't bother him
much; but say, William, you wasn't thinkin' 'bout marriage, was yer? "

" Ya'as I was."

" You was! Do tell! I want ter
know! "

" Ya'as."

" Was you real seerus, William, 'bout
it? "

" Oh! ya'as."

" You air engaged to a young woman
then, I take it."

"Wa'al it's a — more'n that, father."

"What! you ain't gone an' got engaged to two of 'em, have yer?"

At this question William remained silent for fully two minutes; then shaking his head he looked smilingly at the old man and said slowly —

"It's more than a engagement, father; fact is I've gone and got married."

"You married! Wa'al naow, grease up a little, a man don't git married every day. Tell us about it — who's the gal?"

"She worked down there 'n Boston a short time, though she's country born and bred; raised in Farnham."

"I want ter know! Wa'al when all 's said and done, William, I never thot ye'd marry, yer sech a silent rooster I could never see as ye'd screw up talk enough to ask a gal."

"I don't jest say thet I did," piped William, with the ghost of a smile.

"Sho! d'ye mean ter say she popped?"

"Wa'al, father, 'twas done kind o' easy and sudden, naow thet I come to think on't.

She tuk care o' some rooms down there, in a big buildin', for a perfessor who larns folks how to speak pieces; ellercution, she called it. Wa'al I used ter bring in ice every day, an' me an' Araminty used ter talk."

"You don't say, William!"

"Ya'as Araminty used ter talk quite a leetle, an' we struck up a friendship somehow, hed sody water with ice cream in it, an' took some trolley rides of a Sunday. An' one day she says to me, says she, the ice business is a good business, Mr. Julep, says she. 'Twas out in Mount Auburn grave yard, we went out there in them 'lectric cars an' sot a while."

"Wa'al guess that's all father; I didn't say much but we got married yisterday."

"An' I've never heard you talk so much before in all your life. Naow William, I b'lieve Araminty's a woman thet can rise ter the occasion, and thet's jest what you want. Stands ter reason natur must provide fer a leetle difficulty like yourn. Is she a well favored gal?"

" She's right smart, father, she can talk
an' talk.   I never see any one talk like
'Mint.   She can jest talk right on 'thout
thinkin'."

" Thet ain't sech a oncommon 'complish-
ment o' the sex as yer seem ter think;
'specially in courtin' time," observed Tom
eyeing the bridegroom narrowly.

" But I'm glad yer got a woman thet
can talk, she'll need ter.   Where yer
keepin' her? "

" Haow? "

" Where's the gal yer married yisterday — where's yer wife? "

" On her weddin' tower."

" What! hain't she up here along with
you? "

" No she 'hain't."

" Why consarn ye," cried Tom with
sudden warmth, " whatever possessed yer
to do sech a darn fool thing as thet."

" Wa'al 'twas this way, father; I
wanted ter tell my folks, and Mint al-
lowed as how she orter go ter Farnham
an' break the news to the childern."

"What! childern?"

"Oh! I forgot ter say, father, thet Mint's a widder."

"A widder! wa'al ef thet don't beat all, but widders are wise," said Tom, while a broad smile played around the corners of his mouth.

"I've no doubt yer married a good gal, an' I wish yer luck. When are yer goin' ter begin house-keepin'?"

"Mint 'll let me know."

Tom Julep arose and pointing a warning finger at his son, said slowly, "William, don't yer never tell yer mother what yer've jest told me; it might prejudice her agin Araminty, an' naow I'm a goin' ter bed."

CHAPTER II

FARNHAM

My DEER HUSBEND

I now take my pen in hand to let you know that I found sister Anne and the childern well.

I told them I was married but I dont calkelate they are old enought to reelize their nue pa. I dunno as I told you as I had 5 childern. I dunno as you ever ast me. My oldest boy Jimmy is going to be a orrater, you wouldnt think so now cause its orful hard for Jimmy to do anything with his mouth xcept eat, but I'm tryin to cultur him. Its bin disappintin too at times, cause cultur comes hard to Jimmy. Sometimes I think it would be most as easy to cultur one of them injuns front of a seegar store.

11

I onct heard the perfesser tell a man he
war'nt responsive and thats the trouble
with Jimmy, and its the trouble of lots of
folks. I had an ant onct that couldnt
smile; she warnt responsive though some
folks said she was jest savin her face —
well seein it had to stand the ware and tare
of 60 odd years mebbe you couldunt blame
her but she tuck it with her when she went
and no one was sorry. Theres nothin
cheeper on earth than a word onless it be a
smile, and when you meet folks chirrup a
little.   Thats my motto.

Next to Jimmy comes Mamie. She's
reel smart I dont have to squeese talk out
of Mamie — she can make a clothes pin
argy back to her. Next to her comes
Tommy I'm a going to make him one of
them moosicien fellers that teeters on a
brass trumpit.

Last and youngest there meer babies as
yet, come the twins Gresham and Egremont. Thems pretty and high soundin
names, but wait William till you hear the
dredful sekel!

When them twins was born ev'ry body was a hankerin to name 'em. Its supprisin how folks butt in when it comes to namin a baby,— the meenest relashun you've got is willin' to dispense names grattis.

Well tenny rate when the twins come my next door neighbor said I orter call em after a saint,— and Bella Ball, me and her was girls together (awful romancin girl was Bella, married reel well Henry Ball in the soap greese business) well she come to see the twins and she said as how she'd jest read a lovely story about a hero who was dredful wicked but hansom and bold and she wanted to name one of the twins after him.

Now says I them twins are goin to git a name, Bella and I'm agoin to name 'em, —theyre not goin to be called for saint nor sinner, theyre goin to be called for theirselves. O Araminty says Bella in a reel coaxin way, call 'em Gresham and Egremont. It do sound butiful, and I must admit I liked the sound of Gresham and

Egremont from the first. The country is swarmin with Billys and Tommys but of the aforesed there aint so many.

Gresham was a nearl says Bella, and Egremont was a dook, a noble dook. Well I weakened and they was baptised Gresham and Egremont and what's the result; Greshams bin biled down to Ham and Egremont cut off to Eg. Yes William the twins are called Ham and Eg for short and I 'spose its a judgment on me for high soundin names. I dont beleeve in pet names at all. Give a child a pet name and its sure to stick to him through life. There was Boysie Dingwell old and tough and grizzled but jest cause dotin parents rhapsodeezed over him in short pants, he was Boysie to the end of the chapter.

Made no difference that it said on his toomstone

Here lies the body of Jeremiah
Gone to sing in the celestial choir.

Thats what was writ on it at first but

afterwards they was 'fraid folks would-
unt know it was Boysie — you see they'd
spent a lot of money on that toomstone
and twas kind of disapintin to think of
any one having doubts, so tenny rate at
last they had it changed to

Here lieth the bones of Boysie Ding-
well
Gone to join the hosts that sing well.

And now William I must tell you about
our plans — I guess sister Anne is reel
pleased I got you and can take the childern off her.

I tell you what keepin a pair of imps
from takin chances to maim theirselves
for life every hour in the day is no sinch.

Tenny rate Anne has a chance to house
keep for Dave Ward at Farnham Corner
and as he is a widder man it would be flyin
in the face of providence not to go.   Now
I have always wanted to keep a few
lodgers, I calkelate theres money in it and
its me as likes to earn a dollar when I can.

I never told you William that when I

was workin at the prefessers I was injuiced to buy a share of stock in the Great
Beruba Plantation Company. Its a
splendid thing to invest your money in
cause it pays you ten times more than
savings banks.

The share cost $150. This is a orful
lot of money but by payin a little each
month, the agent showed me how i could
git an income for life. Now William I
have in mind a good place to locate, and
when I git suited I'll move all my things
and let you know.

Your lovin wif
Araminta

P. I. L. I hope your pa an ma was
pleesed at your gitting Mint Julep.

CHAPTER III

Wintop

My Deer Husbend (that's to be) I was reel pleased to git your letter and I am glad that you are going to help your pa for a few days.

I got a cottage at Wintop which place is a sort of a little watering pot for Boston. As most all the cottages had a name on, I painted a name on ourn and nailed it over the front door. I heard it onct when I was at the perfessers and I kind o' like the looks of Thanatopsis — I also have got a card up, Rooms to let in my front winder.

My next door neighbor is mister and misses McPeak, a childless couple who have their house just filled with roomers.

17

She is a reel nice spoken woman, and aint it strange William, but yisterday over the back fence we was a talking and she told me she had put some money in that Beruba Plantation too.

She doesnt want Scotty thats her husband, to know it for the world cause he's awful close with money is Scotty, but its nothing venture nothing win with her. She says she's worritting about it cause lately it hasent been paying only about half the devidends it did at first and yet she feels that it will come out all right cause before she ever put her money in it she went to see the manager of the whole thing, a Mister Orrin Feather, with a office on State street where you'd sink in the velvet carpets as was on them floors, and when she told him she had some doubts about its being all he claimed, he sed to her jest go down and see the Plantation for yourself Miss McPeak. He says this is not a gold mine in the Wilds of Alaska, nor a well in the heart of Afric, says he, this is a immens plantation where they raise coffee an rubber an spices an sech like, this is splendid enterprise for you an me to consider an reep the profits, says he, its a big Plantation not far from a thriveing town in Mexico, says he visitors are welcome an your inspection is solicited.

Well as this was pretty fair she bought two shares in this big enterprise. I told her that I was kinder sorry that I had put money in it, for says I, one hundred an fifty dollars would buy an offul lot of coffee, an I dont never wear rubbers, there too drawin on the feet.

Still an income fer life is somethin to try for, an though that looks like offul big profits, I feel its a strate, honest compny.

I had a terrible lesson onct William in a dishonest compny. Did I ever tell you about the shoe string compny William. Well I have jest got to git up from this letter, cause Ham has walked in with a bloody nose an covered with dirt.

I never see sech youngsters for trouble. Its born in them, an I hev strong doubts if they ever grow up hull an connected.

So I will hev to quit this letter William,
but I'll tell you about the shoe string Compny in my next.

                    Your lovin wife
                              Araminta.

CHAPTER IV

"THAT SHOESTRING FELLER"

WINTOP

DEER WILLIAM
I was glad ter hear that you was well, an hope this will find you the same as it leaves me.

There aint any special news, all the folks round here are jest about the same, but William I want ter tell you about that shoe string compny as I promised I would in my last.

Well it struck our town like a syclone an left us about as dazed. Twas this way, a reel nice appearin young man came round one day, smart I tell you, had talk enough to run the country an he went to every house in town. He had a box with three shoe strings in it an a lot of printed dirrections how to make them.

21

We was to buy his box of three shoe strings an the printed dirrections for one dollar, an then make a full box an send it to his address an git five dollars for every box we sent. The boxes was to be sent to the United States army in Hindoostan an a lot of furrin places he menshioned.

Well it looked like a good thing an every one took a box an paid a dollar, myself with the others an though it seemed a lot of money, what was a dollar I argeyed when there was the chanct to make four on every box of them shoe strings.

Well William the shot up of this was our town went shoe string crazy. There was shoe string parties and shoe string clubs; folks talked shoe strings stead of weather.

They forgot old grudges an met each other with a regular shoe string smile. Old Sally Bowen, with a spite agin my Ant Eliza of years standing, met her on the street an asked her how she was gittin on with the shoe strings as nice as could

be. Well bimeby the boxes began to be
sent away an visions of wealth kept folks
awake nights an they was plannin an plot-
tin what they was goin to do when they
got the shoe string money.

Mis Beck who'd sent three boxes, that
was fifteen dollers, and who'd never gone
further than her back gate for twenty
years, was talking of taking a trip to New
York.

Sally Lucas the butchers wife, offul
dressy woman was Sally, said she was tired
to death of home styles an she thought of
goin strate to Paris. Well there we was a
hangin round the post office, waiting for
the wealth to come by return mail like a lot
of childern holding up their hands to a
Christmas Tree.

At last back came the boxes shoe strings
an all, as there wasent any sech address, an
not till then did we reelize that we'd been
taken in.

Well the up shot of the thing was, there
was shoe strings enough in town to lace
up the lower limbs of a nation.

Twas a swindle of the deepest die thats what it was, and Si Banks who had cussed like fury cause he happened to be away the day that smooth chap came round, an who went an tried to buy a box off his wifes niece, well that old Si Banks was jest huggin himself, and told us we'd best make a rope of the shoe strings and hang ourselves for bein sech a lot of Idjits as to buy three shoe strings for a doller.

That sorter cured me of money schemes but wouldnt I jest love to meet that shoe string feller once, fore I die.

Now William I'm keepin my eye on the papers to see if I can find some good place for you to work.

The childern are well.

Yours lovin and waitin
Mint.

Put in later.

A young lady called yisterday to look at a room but my Maymie playin on the steps, told her I was out. Now warnt that too provokin when I was only talkin to Mis McPeak over the back fence.

My Maymie is enough to clip the wings
of Gabriel at times, and she hasent any
tack about her at all.   I have made a hen
coop in the yard and am goin to keep some
hens cause fresh eggs is high in this place
and kinder scarse.

CHAPTER V

GETTING A JOB AND A BOARDER

WINTOP

MY DEER WILLIAM
I have got you work leastwise
I think I have. I read in the
paper that a man was wanted for general
work, on a large estate so I went strait to
the address and saw a mister Ogdin in a
large office in the city. Sir, says I, you
want a good stiddy industrus man to
work about your place dont you — yes
says he, was you thinking of applyin for
the job, yes says I, not for myself, though
I wouldent be afraid to try it says I, but
I came for my William; hes a good stiddy
man, no better living says I, but hes got
one failing, he cant talk and thats all
there is about it.

Not that hes a deef and dummy man

says I, hes dumb from choice not necessitty. The fact is William Julep says jest as few words as its possible for one human to say to another, says I.

Well do you know he looked at me kind of queer and he says my good woman send your William to me.

Now William youve got to leave Little Acres at onct, start immejit, cause theres no time like the present.

I was reel sorry to hear that your ma had ruematiz, she ought to try Bucks Herb Mixture its splendid. There was a pattent medisin feller came to Farnham onct with Bucks Herb Mixture. I disremember the price, but I know that mixture was garanteed to cure anything from a ingrowin toe nail, to hydrofoby itself — it would put whiskers on men and take them off wimmen, and Ill never forget the case of Jane Witherspoon, Jane was invallid for years, had akes and panes in every part of her annatommy, besides the simpathy of the publick at large, it is true William that at a meetin onct when a bad boy hollered fire Jane forgot her crutches and was the fust to land safe in the street — but that aint the pint. Jane Wither-spoon bought a bottle of Bucks Herb Mixture and she was assured by the med-isin feller, that at the end of a week she could hang up one krutch with imputeny, at the end of the second she could hang up the other with a cleer conshense and at the end of the third she could hang up the family wash with resignashion.

Now William I will close hoping that soon you will be home with your lovin wife and childern and if your folks should think you are going away too soon from them speek up smart William, and tell em the time has come when you must leave your pa and ma for your own lovin
                              MINT JULEP

Put in later.

I am learning Jimmy to make a perlite bow and charge of the Light Brigade, its hard — I have to threaten Jimmy to keep his hands outer his pockits, but Im bound my childern will git cultur if I have to cultur them with a broom stick.

WINTOP.

MY DEER WILLIAM

It doo seem as if fate was again us livin together in the holey bonds of wedloc for any considrable time.

I never thot that mister Ogdin would take you away out to hunt in them Rocky Mountings, when you had only been with him sech a short time. He seems to have taken quite a likin to you which dont surprise me, seein as I did myself. Tenny rate I bet he admires you cause you are a strong and fearfull man and can keep your mouth shet.

I have a feelin that he admires to have you go jest cause you dont talk. Well that may be good and then again it may not.

Some one has got to do the talkin in this world and talkin can do a few things. There was Johnny Speers, lived alongside us in Farnham, a pesky little rooster, allus bumpin himself again some one, and one day he went to town and bumped himself again a car — his little carcass might a got a good stirrin up but no more an that, well do you know one of them lawyer fellers tuk the case to court an got a pile of money. Was you hurt much Johnny says I when the hull thing was over. Well, says Johnny, I dident reckon I was near so much till thet lawyer stud up an then evry bone in my body was a cryin to heaven for damages.

Talk done that, William — jest plain jaw work. An now William I hope you will be karefull — look out for wild beests. I shouldent go ramblin round alone at night if I was you, and dont forgit your

MINT JULEP.

Put in later

I havent let one room yet in Thanatopsis. I spose its the childern. Most people dont hanker to take on five promiscus all to onct.

WINTOP.

DEER WILLIAM .

I now take my pen in hand to let you know that your wife and family are well an it is nearly two weeks sense I heard from you. I have been worriting, William, look out for wild animils.

Theres a roomer at last in Thanatopsis. A young lady pretty as a pioney an do you know William thet I have made the strange diskovery that a mistery is a hangin over her.

What it is I cant yit say but theres somethin ailin that gal or my name hasent been changed from Allum to Julep.

I says to her the other day, says I, scuse me Miss Burt, her name is Molly Burt, be you reel well says I, an she says to me in that sweet way of hern, why thank you Mis Julep says she, I'm very well.

But theres a kind of sadness about her, an yisterday I ran acrost her settin alone, and if she warnt weepin I'm tung tied.

I've got to quit writin now, so I will

close hopeing soon I'll git a letter from you to your own

MINT JULEP.

Put in later:

Mr. Voneye a reel estate little German man wot rooms at McPeaks and who rented me Thanatopsis is goin to give Tommy twenty lessons on the trumpit fer fresh eggs.

Them hens warnt a bad investmint.

CHAPTER VI

ABOUT CHOOSING A HUSBAND

A CLICK of the gate one bright morning made the two neighbors, who were indulging in a friendly chat at the fence, glance up quickly, to see the new roomer at Thanatopsis just going out.

"There's Miss Burt," said Mint, "I think she's 'most the prettiest gal I ever see, an' better nor that, she's jest as nice as she's pretty."

"She is a guid looking lass as ever I see," said Mrs. McPeak as she looked admiringly after Molly.

"But there's somethin' wrong," said Mint in an undertone, "there's a mystery about that gal as sure as your name is McPeak."

"What-ever makes ye think thot, Mrs. Julep?"

"Everything makes me think it, Mrs. McPeak. What is a gal like her doin', livin' like this, jest look at her clo'es, they are not showy nor gay, not at all, but they are the very finest quality, Mrs. McPeak, and she wears them like a queen. She ain't no ordinary gal, it's plain to see that; she's a lady born and bred but there's something gone wrong, for she's not feeling happy — anyone can see that."

"P'r'aps she is in love, Mrs. Julep."

"In love! why bless yer that wouldn't make a gal look sad an' yaller. When a gal's in love, she's bloomin' as a mornin' glory, thinks the whole world's heaven, an' her young man a little better than the angels."

"Well it may be that the course of true love ain't running smooth, Mrs. Julep."

"O! of course if there's any trouble or misunderstandin', I s'pose it's different. I'd like to give gals some good motherly

advice on love and matrimony, for when
love gits into the heart, common sense
flies outer the head of lots of gals.
Most gals don't go the right way about
matrimony, anyhow."

"It's a foolish age, Mrs. Julep, and
ye can't expect too much of a gal when
she's in love."

"Well, if a gal wants to git married,
an' that's the lot of most of 'em, not but
what a single woman has much to be
thankful fer, but if a gal wants a husband,
then says I, let her go about it in a busi-
ness-like way. If a gal is goin' to git
a new dress she don't take any old thing,
nor yit the fust cloth she looks at allus.
She goes 'round a little and spends some
time lookin'; she looks at the color and
the weave, finds out if it will wash and
wear well, and if it will shrink from water,
and a whole lot more 'fore she'll make up
her mind to take it.

"Now it do seem to me no more than
reasonable that she be willin' to spend as

much thought on the man she's goin' to take fer the rest of her life.

"Let her find out his price, how much he can earn; let her look at the weave and the color, that's whether he's a decent, God fearin', religious man, or one of them light fingered, flip-tongued scoffers that has no religion hisself, but tries to take away everybody else's, and let her find out above all if he shrinks from water. If more gals 'ud find that out 'fore they married, it would save heaps of misery afterward.

"I've no patience with shilly-shallyin' gals that set down waitin' for the fust thing that might grow whiskers, to come along and ask them. Didn't the good Lord give them a tongue and all the minor senses? Well He did and He expects 'em to use it, and there's no word in the Bible agin a woman findin' a good husband, for just look at Ruth, the Moabitess, and how she found Boaz.

"My advice to gals is, if you want a good husband, jest look round till he finds you, and you can help him if he's not good at findin'.

" When I was twenty I didn't have them sentiments, if I did, mebbe I wouldn't be Mint Julep to-day, though yer can't allus tell."

" That ye can't, Mrs. Julep, for they do say as ye'll get what's laid out for ye."

" Well, as fur as that goes, my grandmother used ter say if a gal set in the corner all her life, her fate 'ud walk in some day an' set in the oppsite corner; mebbe 'twas ordered fer folks to play puss in the corner for a mate, but I have my doubts.

" When I was eighteen, one of my brother Hiram's walkin' mates used ter set a heap by my cake and biscuit, and there's no knowin' what might 'a happened if I'd egged him on a little after a good meal, but I didn't, never — an' when I was about twenty there was a man with nine childern in our town who walked home from church with me, strait to the door, the first Sunday he 'peared out as a widder man, but I warn't a bit spunky in those days an' a reddy made family has its drawbacks well as its advantages. But I learned to look at things diffrent later an' when big Tom Evans came 'round castin' sheep eyes at Matildy, I up an' clinched the matter right then an' thar.

"Matildy was the youngest of all of us an' looked on me as her mother — a right good gal she was, an' pretty as a piny. She was awful bashfull an' Tom was more so, but he managed to stalk inter the house seven nights a week an' set thar a chewin' a straw.

"That state of affairs kept on fer three months, an' then one night I sent Matildy to Ant Liza's a purpose an' I swooped down on Tom after he'd settled comfortably in the best chair an' begun to chew his straw. 'Tom,' says I, 'yer cheatin' some poor hoss outer a lot of good feed — why not git married an' save the hay. In other words,' says I, 'what's yer intenshions, if I might ask, toward Matildy.'

"Well, Tom looked as if he was goin' to fall all in a heep. 'I ain't a meenin' any harm,' says Tom, scairt to death — 'Then yer must be meanin' matrimoney,' says I, ''cause anything else would be harm after takin' up a gal's time fer three months.'

"Well, Tom had sense an' was manly spite of his grass chewin', an' tenny rate, him an' Matildy got married that spring. If a man hasent any intents or purpose toward matrimoney then he'd better not go callin' steddy on a gal till he has, an' if he has intents, he knows it jest as well in three months as twelve — so what's the good of wastin' ile, an' wearin' out the parlor furnitoor.

"'Nother thing I've noticed, when they're coortin', folks allus keep the best side out, an' it's perfeckly proper thet they should, but there'd be a lot more successful matches, if they'd continue to keep the best side out after marriage. Some way or other men are awful human an' I don't blame 'em lots of times. If it warn't fer the men the world wouldn't be as round as they say 'tis. At the same time I do hope thet sweet Miss Burt ain't wearin' her heart out fer any man — she can git along without the man, but she can't without the heart, an' there never was a man yit on this blessed earth, a mite too good fer a good woman.

"Matein' is queer any way you look at it. Gals thet like tall men, git short ones — an' those thet 'ud fancy flesh, are more than apt to have to take skin an' bone.

"From the time I calkelated on man as a mate, I allus did admire one thet could blow a brass trumpit, bow to the ladies an' make a perlite speech. Good lands, d'ye see what I got — my first husband, Jamesy Allum, was a little deef, an' my second is all but dumb, not but there's wuss men than William Julep, an' I doo think William is good lookin', though he seems pessesed to greese his hair an' now I have got to go, Mis Mc-Peak. I have stayed talkin' too long."

CHAPTER VII

" WRITE AT ONCT "

WINTOP

DEER WILLIAM:
Its now three weeks sense I heard from you an if you don't write at onct, I'll start for them Rockey Mountings immejit, else how can I know thet you are alive in sech compny.

The least any woman can know about herself is whether she be maid wife or widder. Write at onct an dont make it so pesky short.

Your wife,
ARAMINTA JULEP.

P. i. l.

My Jimmy is doin' splendid, he has learned to say his piece reel well, he will resite it fer you when you git home.

41

CHAPTER VIII

"WELL, Miss Burt, it do seem as if I was allus bumpin' into you when you was writin' in that little book. All the time I was gettin' my vegetables ready fer dinner, I could look right through the settin' room an' see you on the porch, writin' away."

" I keep a diary," laughed Molly, " did you ever keep one, Mrs. Julep? "

" Keep a diry! never! If yer do a good thing you'll remember it, an' if yer do a foolish one, yer friends won't let yer forgit it — you'll be reminded either way so wot's the use of writin' it down."

" There's a good bit of philosophy in that, Mrs. Julep," said Molly with a smile.

" I remember though the fust time I ever heard tell of a diry," Mint went on.

42

" I had a friend onct, Bella. Awful
romancin' gal was Bella, married reel
well in the soap greese bisness, an' one day
she told me she was goin' to keep a diry.
I didn't tell you that Bella was one of
nine, loafin' on her dad who uster sell milk
in Farnham, did I. Well, 'tenny rate, I
thought Bella was goin' to put in an' do
some work, instead of which she pulls out
a little black book — 'everything I do in
the coorse of the day,' says Bella, ' I'm
goin' to write down here. This is what
happened yisterday,' says she, an' she began to read like this:

" ' Pleasant day, I riz at six, et pie an'
coffee, went out, met a man, he looked
right at me,' an' so on. ' Is thet a diry,
Bella?' says I, when she got so far as puttin' her front hair up in papers, an' lamp
out fer the night. ' Yes,' says Bella, ' ain't
it a cute idee?' ' It'd be a handy thing to
put alongside of your corpse,' says I, ' all
you'd have to do on the other side would
be to pass it to the recordin' angel, and
save him the time of lookin' you up.'

"What's the good of writin' down all the fiddle faddles of life anyhow, it seems to me a sensible person will forgit them as quick as he can. The Bible is my diry — I've got writ down the day and date of my marriage to William Julep, not that I'm likely to forgit it, which is more'n I'd vouch for him, an' my childern's births; as for weather. the Bible records quite a storm in Noah's time — it's the only storm for Christians to remember. No, I can't say that I believe in diries, Miss Burt."

"Well, my mother kept one, and my grandmother did also. I think," said Molly, by way of apology, "that it runs in the family to keep a diary."

"There's lots of things run in families thet orter be run out. Take my brother Hiram, he used ter play hookey from school when he was a lad, an' was allus wanderin' off, 'specially when there was any work to do — he never forgot to turn up at meal time though; well, he grew to be a stiddy shirker, an' mother used ter

say, same as if 'twas somethin' to be cocked
up about, ' Oh well, gran'pa was a great
traveller, it runs in the family,' and then
Hiram would go off again.

"Well, Hiram had a impedalment in
his speech, an' stuttered somethin' offul
when he got mad. Why, he used to git
so riled up, the words would jest stick in
his thrut, and then he had a pecooliar habit
of raisin' his leg to sorter help him git
them out.

"Well, one day poor mother died, and
the burden of Hiram and a household fell
on me. I uster lay awake at nights,
thinkin' of Hiram's case — there was no
use scoldin' or appealin' to his pride, 'cause
he hed none.

"Onct I told him thet he was loosin'
his looks, folks uster call him handsome,
and most every one has a vanity spot
somewhere, an' you can hit a lot of people
on that spot.

"But Hiram didn't, all he had was a
good appetite, an' a spite fer work.

"Well, at last I hit on a desprit plan.

I hed a fit one night, outside his door, an'
he was scairt to death, an' the next day
I was terrible sick an' made him promise
not to leave me an' whenever I see him
gettin' restless, I'd jest drop off inter one
of them fits, an' when I came out I'd tell
him I wasn't goin' to last long an' I'd
will him the ten acre lot, thet was mine
from Aunt Mary.   Well, to make a long
story short, Hiram stayed on till he got
so dead sick of the house, he came one
day an' told me he'd half a mind to go
to work fer John Barnes, who needed an
extry man.

"'Go, Hiram,' says I, martyr like,
'you're a young man an' I don't want ter
be interferin' with yer prospects.'   Thet
was a good thing fer me an' better still fer
Hiram — John Barnes shook some of the
laziness outer him, then he married Peggy
Barnes, an' she done the rest, for he never
travelled forty feet from his own door you
bet, without Peggy.

"Yes, there's many a fault an' bad
habit that folks saddle off on some harm-

less member of the family thet's dead an'
gone, an' can't rise up to contradic' them.

"I don't see the sense of keepin' lots
of things thet folks keep, anyhow — Take
clothes, if folks would take down some of
the clothes thet's hangin' on a peg, an'
hang them on some poor human, the world
would look better an' so would the clothes.
There's my purple silk, I give you my
word, Miss Burt, I never was one thet
titivated more'n the average, but I allus
did want a purple silk. I uster think if
I could sweep down the aisle of a Sabbath,
an' know thet a shimmerin' purple was
rustlin' at every step, I could defy Satan
an' all his coworts — visions of thet silk
uster come between me an' my chanct of
heaven in them days. Well I got it, an'
now it's put away in musk, I'm 'most
ashamed to say.

"Some folks are allus hoardin' anyway.
It's mighty thoughtful for them thet gits
the hoardin's. I knew a woman onct thet
uster drink her tea outer an old cracked
chiny cup, though she hed a beautiful tea

set in her closet thet she was hoardin'.
When she died, her niece, Lyddy Deane,
got it an' she uster show it to folks, an'
they uster say my! ain't it beautiful, an'
all thet, an' there they was a praisin' thet
chiny tea set, but not one word fer the old
lady that hoarded it all them years.

"When I die, nobody's goin' to praise
my chiny more'n they praise me, not if I
know it — though there might be somethin' in what Lyddy said to me onct:
'Do you know, Araminty,' says she,
'every time I look at thet chiny, I think
of thet dear old soul, an' I'm sure she
still takes an intrust in it. Sometimes,'
says she, 'when I'm settin' alone an' pour-
in' tea, I see her kind old face a smilin'
at me opposite, an' she's sippin' her tea
outer thet little rose cup.'

"Lyddy was an awful sweet gal an'
I'm glad she got thet rose chiny, but I hed
my doubts about the old lady a drinkin'
outer it."

"Oh! I never could do it," said Molly.
"There are some things I couldn't give

away, there's Cleopatra, green, gauzy, and alluring, I wore it two years ago, but I simply couldn't give Cleopatra away. And there's the Dawn, soft, uncertain, pale as gray sea mist. I love the Dawn, Mrs. Julep, though I wore it ever so long ago. Why! I have The Maiden's Prayer put away in lavender; I name all my gowns and The Maiden's Prayer was my graduating dress. Oh! Mrs. Julep, I'm a romancer, I fear."

"Well, you are romancin' to name your old gowns sech hifalutin' names, but I dunno as you're a patch on Bella Ball.

"Bella was the most romancin' gal I ever see — Why, anything thet grew hair on the upper lip sent little shivers down Bella's back.

"I remember onct, me an' Bella was mere gals at the time, an we went up one day to Hitchcock's farm, to git fresh eggs, an' we found a new man to wait on us up there; Stillman B. Wickford, fresh from Maine; an' like all the folks I ever see from there, he warn't hidin' his lights.

"Well, we talked casiel like, about crops an' weather, an' when we was a goin' Bella looks back over my shoulder, an', says she, real sweet, 'O-ra-ver, Mister Wickford,' thet's the furrin fer good day. Well, the very next day she got a letter from Stillman B., saying as how her image hed been constant in his heart an' askin' her to appint a time an' place of meetin'. Well, Bella had like to die a laffin'; 'twas her first love letter, an' mebbe 'twas the last, 'cause Henery Ball was stronger on greese than he was on paper, not but what he could reed an' write some.

"'Tenny rate, I talked Bella outer meetin' a clandestin man, so she didn't take no notice, though her vanity was tickled, you can bet.

"Well, 'bout a week later we both went agin to buy more eggs. We reeched Hitchcock's big kitchen an' I know Bella's heart was goin' pitty pat, an' when we knocked some one said come in, an' in we stept, an' there sat Stillman B. a washin' his feet in a tub of water.

" She turned her back on him an' looked outer the winder, but I could see him from the corner of my eye, mop his extremes as unconsarned as if he was a curryin' a hoss, an' when he gits good an' ready he gits up an' git us the eggs. But, law, Miss Burt, do you think thet cured Bella? Bless you, no. She asked me on the way home if he warn't hansom an' bold, an' I allowed as he certainly hed courage to wash in publick.

" I uster think Bella would loose her romancin' when she lost her waist line; most women do, but she never did. Some females 'ud see a romance in a wooden post if there was a man's coat hangin' on it.

" An' now I must quit talkin', and see about gittin' my dinner on."

CHAPTER IX

DEER AN WELL BELOVID HUSBEND:
I was glad to git your letter,
though I will say I'd be ashamed
to write sech a short one, even to a under-
taker.

But I know your failin William, an
you cant write cause writin is only talkin on paper.

Well, me an Miss Burt are gittin reel
soshiable, though I havent yit found out
a inklin of the mistery. The other day
she says to me, says she, what a busy
woman you are, Mis Julep; time never
hangs heavy on your hands, does it? No,
you bet it dont, says I; some folks has so
much time they dont know what to do
with theirselves, an others has so little
thet they never git a chanct to set down an

52

git reel well acquainted with theirselves.
I sometimes think if I hed a chanct to set
down an' git reel well acquainted with
Araminta Julep, I might find something
interestin to her besides washin, churnin,
bakin, an mendin. As it is, she's sech a
rushin, crushin, disapintin critter I cant
abide her, an I often wished I could a done
somethin of some account. O, you
musent say that, says miss Burt, think
what a splendid usefull life you live, says
she, workin an' thinkin an' plannin for
others. Thet may be says I but Ive hed
longings all my life to do somethin big-
ger an better. I aint done them an we
dont git credit jest fer the longings.
Well I'm not so sure of thet, says miss
Molly, an then she says in her prettiest
way, says she,

> All I could never be
> All men ignored in me,
> This I was worth to God.

I thought it was so nice an poetkal
like, thet I asked her if she'd jest as soon

put it down on paper fer me. I have allus liked poetkal things though I never hed a chanct to do much in thet line.

Night before last miss Burt invited me to a sing in a big hall. It was nice, but the women dident speak plain I couldent understand one word. I was jest longin fer some one to come out an sing home, sweet home, or old oaken buckit. I was jest wishin we was at the show. How I love a show, though I never go — but I see a great actress once, her name was Sary somethin. I was at the perfessers at the time an a gentleman what uster come there gave me a ticket an I went an I'll never forgit it to my dyin day; it was grand. The name of the show was Frow-Frow; thets furrin for two wives. I dont know what twas all about cause she was a furriner, but I took it she was a decent sort but the rest was jest mormons an wuss. But she hed a voice thet sent little thrills up an down yer marrer, an I set on the edge of my chair holdin my breath most of the time.

Well tenny rate I guess she'd been flyin round hevin a good time, an her constitootion wouldent stand it so the poor thing tuk to her bed at last. I knew in a minit what ailed thet woman, an the more I looked at her the wuss I felt, an I says to the woman settin next to me, says I, if some one would only tell her to take some camomile tea, a good dose of camomile tea, she'd be outer thet bed in no time, says I.

Well thet woman whispered it to the man settin alongside of her, an he said he'd tell her soon as the show was over, but do you know them unfeelin folks sot there an jest clapt an shouted till thet poor thing hed to git outer thet sick bed, an drag herself fore the curtain an told them she was much obliged an feelin better when all the time she looked as white an wasted as a wilted calla. I was jest thet mad I felt spiteful gainst the hull crowd.

Thet was the only time I was ever in a reel play house, though there was onct

in our town a compny thet played Uncle
Toms Cabin, but it warnt a success.
Hicks Bosworth got mad at a black whiskered feller struttin round in cow hide
boots flourishin a whip. Hicks stud
right up in the show an offered to lick
him. It made an awful commotion, but
Hicks was six foot one in his socks, an
when the boys began to urge him on an
throw things at the actor folks, they rung
down thet curtain an the show sneaked
outer town thet night, but old Si Banks
what kept the hotel said they was awful
mad an they left a big notice over the
door of the town hall in red paint; it said
somethin like this: If Hicks Bosworth
would stand up before a baby jackass,
we'll back the jackass fer the brains an
blows, an a whole lot more. I guess
every one of them gave us a dig.

They called us puddin heads, an pie
eaters an it riled up Hicks so he found
out where they was playin two nights
after an he sent a notice an paid a man
to reed it right out loud in the show thet

said,— Hicks Bosworth of Farnham is willin an anxsious to meet the Jackass of this show, an Hicks would like to borrer the weapon the aforesaid jackass carries around thets commonly used on his kind.

They said it spoiled the show in thet town too. Folks dident allus approve of Hicks. He was like a overheeted furnase, ready to bust any minnit. But what made him so mad at thet play acter was cause Susie Hobbs was a settin right down in the front row an he thot the black whiskered feller was showin off an throwin glances at her but if he was, Susie was willin to ketch all thet was comin her way an return them with intrust. We all knowed Susie, all but poor Hicks, an he found her out but not before she spiled a good mans life.

I hate a flirt, there the meanest kind of a theif, cause they often steel what cant be replaced. Susie thot all men livin was made to be the victim of her wiles an graces. Now Bella Ball was diffrent. She thot all men jest lovely, an among

the crowd was one pertickler, made a purpose for her, so she was awful nice to all
for fear of missin her pertickler. I cant
think of no more at present, but rite soon
to your own

MINT JULEP.

P. i. l.

Tommy ıs learnin to teeter beautifull
on thet trumpet.

CHAPTER X

WINTOP

Deer WILLIAM
    I was reel glad to see you answered my last so quick.

We are all well, though the twins cant sit down without pain in consequence of slidin down McPeaks cellar door thet hed a small nail inwisible. And this reminds me thet poor mis McPeak is worritin awful about thet money she put in the Beruba Plantation company.

The company dont pay a cent of devidends now, an she's afraid shell lose her money, an wuss nor all, she's afraid Scotty will find it out. She said she wished she knowed a good honest lawyer to put the case in his hands but she dident know one. She says honest lawyers aint so

59

plenty, an I told her I dident know any seein as I was a stranger in these parts but I'd ask miss Burt if she might know one. Well William it do beet all but thet gal jest blushed like a biled beet when I ast her an says she, yes, I know one both honest and clever, an then I ast her his name an address. Twas Mister Jeremiah Storey, but when I said I'd tell miss McPeak to go strait to him she said O please dont, blushin more an more. Well I was so supprised I jest looked at her an I says, I understand miss Burt, says I, thet mister Jeremiah is a good honest lawyer but no dout you hev a good reeson fer not wantin him to help poor miss McPeak. Then she says, no I hev no reeson at all, tell your neighber thet she can trust him above all men. Well now William aint thet the most peeculiar thing you ever herd tell of. Am I gettin on the track of the mistery? What has this lawyer feller got to do with Molly Burt? That is what is puzzlin me.

Tenny rate misses McPeak is goin to

see him an ask him a few questions about
if he thinks we can git our money back
outer thet Beruba Plantation, cause she's
most worriet herself inter a sick bed.

Your own
Mint Julep.

P. i. l.— Tommy is learnin to play
home sweet home on the trumpit.

CHAPTER XI

IT was Saturday afternoon. A knock on the kitchen door made Mrs. Julep pause in the midst of her scrubbing, but before she could get to her feet, the door opened and Mrs. McPeak appeared.

One glance at her neighbor showed Mrs. Julep that something was amiss. The woman's eyes were swollen and red from weeping, and she stood hesitatingly in the doorway, clutching her gingham apron.

"Why, what on earth's the matter? What's troublin' yer? Set down, woman, dear," said Mint, but so astonished that she made no attempt to arise from her knees.

"Oh! Mrs. Julep," moaned the little woman, dropping listlessly into a chair, and covering her eyes with her small, plump hands, " I've lost the money, I've lost the money, an' Scotty 'll kill me."

" He'll do nothin' of the sort," declared Mrs. Julep, sitting back on her heels.

"Oh! yer don't know Scotty, Mrs. Julep; he's a good man, but he's got an awfu' temper, an' he's close; Scotty's awfu' close, an' it'll make him fair wild when he finds out the money's gone.   Oh, what shall I say to Scotty? "

The tears started afresh and trickled down the poor tear-stained cheeks, while she tried to wipe them away with the corner of her apron.

" Well, neighbor, don't loose courage like that; it can't be as bad as you think."

" It could na be worse, Mrs. Julep. It was all a swindlin' scheme ter get money from simple folk that trusted 'em and had faith in 'em, and I believed every word that man Feather told me about that plantation.

" Didn't he tell me I could go down and see it for mysel', and when the first money came in the letter, that was the devidend on what I had paid in, I was that pleased I came near tellin' Scotty, and I wish I had, 'cause then he'd know somethin' about it; but now to hear it all at once 'll make him fair wild. Oh! what shall I say to Scotty!"

"Well, are you sure that the money's gone, Mrs. McPeak?"

"Oh! yes, on the advice of the lawyer, Mr. Storey, I took a car and went down to the place this mornin' and I found lots of others, men and women, askin' fer their money, but they won't give us back a cent. They said as how nothin' can be done until the directors has a meetin', but it's not much good that'll do us, I fear."

"Well, Mrs. McPeak, them directors is mighty smart men, and no knowing but they may be able to do something fer the poor people as trusted in 'em. While there's life in our bodies, there's hope in our hearts, and it mayn't be as bad as it seems."

"Oh! dear, dear, to think of me puttin' Scotty's hard-earned money into sech a wild-cat scheme. Oh, what shall I say to him! The devidend they sent out in the letter was jest a trick ter make folks think they'd be gettin' more if they'd buy more. I see it all now. Oh! what shall I say to Scotty? I dare na face him after throwin' away his good money in sech a foolish thing; he'll kill me. Scotty'll kill me."

"He'll do nothin' of the sort, I tell yer," said Mint, who had been unusually quiet during the woman's outburst.

"You must spunk up a bit and we'll see what can be done. Now, first of all, how much money did you put inter this Beruba business?"

"Three hundred dollars; that was two shares," said Mrs. McPeak, who was calmer now that she was talking it over.

"Three hundred dollars," repeated Mint. "My lands, that's an awful lot of money! My case ain't near so bad. I took one of them shares, but I've only paid in fifty-five dollars on it; but that's jest fifty-five dollars more than I can afford to lose. But three hundred! It's a heap of money, there's no denyin' of that."

"It is, it is," and once more the voice
was shaking with sobs.   " Scotty gives me
every cent to save, and I keep it in a little
place in the bottom of my trunk; he don't
trust no banks, and he's been savin' till
he'd have enough some day to buy a piece
of land.   Oh, my! Oh, my!   Many's the
time we've talked it over and he told me
that when we had enough to buy the land
outright he was goin' to raise a mortgage
and build a house.   And I've lain awake
nights thinkin' how pleased he'd be when
he see the extry money I'd made by my
investment; but now I canna face him.
I'd rather die!   Oh! I could ha' thrown
mysel' in the river, I was that heart broke
this mornin'.   What shall I do and what
shall I say to Scotty!"

"Well, three hundred dollars is an awful lot of money, I admit, Mrs. McPeak,
but a good wife's worth more'n that, and
what you did, you done fer the best, same
as me; we'll make an awful plucky fight to
git our money back, but if it's gone and

we can't git it back, then say I, let it go and be thankful it's no wuss."

"Oh! but Scotty, Mrs. Julep; ye dinna know Scotty. He'll nay listen to any excuse when he finds his good money's gone. I dare na face him. Oh, Mrs. Julep, what shall I do, what shall I do!" and Mrs. McPeak rocked back and forth in the extremity of her woe and looked beseechingly at the woman on her heels before her.

Mrs. Julep looked thoughtfully at the pail of suds by her side; she realized that something must be done to help this unhappy woman, although she could not understand the fear and dread that Mrs. McPeak had of telling her husband about the loss of the money.

Giving two spots in front of the sink a vigorous scrub, she threw the brush on the little shelf above and proceeded to wring out her floor-cloth; she wiped this last portion of the floor quickly, and then, jumping to her feet, stood with hands on her hips and leaned against the old-fashioned sink.

"Well, Mrs. McPeak, I suppose everybody on this green earth sometime is bound to lose good money in a bad venture. I met my shoe-string man and you've met yourn. However, I believe you can git inspiration from soap suds if you're lookin' fer it, and right now in that very pail of suds I've jest seen a way that I can help you out of this."

"Oh! Mrs. Julep, ye canna help me get the money, and it's nothin' less would satisfy Scotty. Oh, what shall I say to him, what shall —"

"*You'll* say nothin' to him," interrupted Mint. "I'll see Scotty McPeak when he comes home to-night and I'll tell him what he ought ter know."

Mrs. McPeak shook her head sadly at this suggestion, but Mint was now thoroughly warmed up to the new role she was about to take upon herself, and continued:

"When your husband comes home to his nice comfortable house to-night, to have his nice warm supper, he'll be dissapinted fer the first time in his life; and instid of a

lovin' wife ter meet him, he'll find it
empty; leastwise it shall be empty 'till I go
over there and set him thinkin' on the right
track."

"Now, Mrs. McPeak, is there anything
special your man likes fer tea?"

Mrs. McPeak looked blankly at her resourceful neighbor, a bewildered expres-
sion in her mild, blue eyes.

"He has a sweet tooth, has Scotty; I've
known him to eat scones and jam wi' a
boy's relish."

"Then it's scones and jam fer tea to-
night, Mrs. McPeak, and you go right
ahead and make the scones, and I'll bring
McPeak back with me fer company to tea.
Don't you stir outer this house till he takes
yer, and don't yer cry any more over that
money; let it go. You've got ter mind
Ham and Eg while I'm gittin' McPeak,
and them twins 'll keep you from broodin'
overmuch on yer trouble jest now."

Mrs. Julep started for the door leading into the back hall, and turning saw
that Mrs. McPeak had not changed her

position and had made no attempt to put
into practise Mint's plan of softening
Scotty's heart.

" Come, now, stir yourself, Mrs. Mc-
Peak, and you leave this thing to me; I've
tackled worse than your Scotty, and when
he finds you've got his favorite dish fer
tea, it'll make him feel so good he won't
mind the old money. Now, you start in
this minute and make the scones; lucky
I've got a bit of jam left that old Mother
Allum sent me last fall; she'll never put up
no more jam, poor old lady, though 'twas
good enough to tempt the saints she's
jined in heaven. You can give the twins
their supper if I ain't back — a bowl of
bread and milk is all Gresham and Egremont git, and then they go straight ter
bed. If they holler, let 'em go it, only
take a peep now and then ter see that
stranglation don't set in."

Mint washed and dried her hands
quickly, and as Mrs. McPeak still remained in the chair, the energetic Mint
bustled into the pantry, brought out flour

and butter, which she placed on the kitchen table, hoping thus to get Mrs. McPeak started on the scones and likewise divert her mind from her great trouble.

" Now, I won't have any more'n time to git ready, and you can go right ahead and make them scones, fer I'm goin' ter bring company back to tea, and —"

" Nay, nay, Mrs. Julep," interrupted the woman, " I'm not sa sure that ye'll bring the mon from his own house; he's that set about things, it's awfu'," and the tears started again.

" There, now, don't think about it any more; if you watch them twins of mine, takin' chances ter maim theirselves fer life, four minutes outer five, you won't be broodin' on yer trouble. I'll run upstairs and jest slip my black skirt over this, then I'm ready. There ain't much of the faint heart, nor likewise the fair lady about me."

Mint rushed upstairs and in a few minutes returned to the kitchen to find Mrs. McPeak standing on tiptoe, peaking out of the window, while behind her the twins were playing soldier, marching up and down the room, with the pan of dough for a drum.

"I've been watching for Scotty," whispered the little woman; "it's most time he was comin'; he gets home earlier on Saturdays. There he is, there he is, jest gone in the door.'

"Oh, Mrs. Julep, I'm afeared; you're meanin' well, but it's not the thing wi' Scotty. It'll make him madder to know that ye know it. Oh! dinna ye go, Mrs. Julep; I'm afeared of Scotty."

All the woman's fears returned with a rush when she caught sight of the redoubtable McPeak entering the seclusion of his own door. She sank into a chair and wept, clasping and unclasping her hands, the very picture of despair.

Mrs. Julep put on her bonnet and shawl hastily, and bidding the woman to "spunk up" and watch the twins and make the scones, she departed.

In answer to Mrs. Julep's short knock,

McPeak presently appeared, looking anything but pleased at the sight of his visitor. He returned her pleasant greeting sullenly and held the door, waiting for her to tell her errand and depart.

" I want ter come in a minute, Mr. McPeak; I hev somethin' ter tell yer' bout yer wife."

She swept past him into the neat little kitchen and opening her bonnet strings, dropped into a chair.

The man closed the door and turned to her in silence.

" I'm awful sorry fer you, McPeak, but I didn't come here to offer sympathy."

" Is — is onything wrong wi' Jennie? "

Mrs. Julep tightened her lips and bowed her head.

" Somethin' is wrong with your wife, Mr. McPeak — everything's wrong with her."

" Gord! hes there been a accident — is she hurtit — is she dead — speak up, woman, where's Jennie?"

" She's not dead nor hurt the way you

mean — she's alive and well; her body's all right, but her head, Mr. McPeak; her head! Oh! that poor woman's head!"

"What's the matter wi' her head — hes she gone daffy? Gord! you set there blabbin' 'bout her head as if 'twas a bloomin' punk she'd dropped on the rod side; what's ailin' her, woman?"

If Mint was at all cast down by the testy Scot, she did not show it in word or look.

"See here, Mr. McPeak, I've come ter prepare yer for a terrible loss, but I'll not say a word till yer tell me what yer wife's wuth; how much is she wuth ter you in dollars and cents — jest tell me that."

For a moment Scotty regarded the woman suspiciously; she had always had too glib a tongue to suit him. But now he began to entertain doubts as to her sanity.

He edged a little nearer the door, and put his hand on the knob. Scotty was cautious, and he wasn't going to take any chances. Mint saw the movement, and the meaning of his act flashed upon her.

" Scotty McPeak, I'm not crazy; I'm usin' sech brains as the Lord gave me fer a purpose. You may have more'n me, but no one's found it out yit. You tell me what your wife is wuth to you in cash, and I'll tell you what yer ought ter know."

" Why, dom it, woman, a mon don't value his wife like thot — ha' ye gone daft that ye ask sich a question?"

" McPeak, you're right — you've got a good wife, and, as the Bible says, her price is above rubies; so yer can't put a value on her in dollars and cents, can yer? A good honest, sober, industrious woman that thinks, and plans and saves fer you every day o' her life, and everything she does, Mr. McPeak, she does fer the best, don't forgit that; when she saves yer money, she saves it fer the best, and if she lost it, she lost it fer the best. What good, say I, would a few hundred dollars be ter you if Jennie was sick or sore, or wuss, laid away fer ever more. 'Twould be a

long time 'fore you'd find another as good.
There's lots of females in the world, Mr.
McPeak; swarms of them, but when you
meet a woman, it's some different. Jennie
did everything for the best, and when she
invested that three hundred dollars, she
thot 'twas fer the best."

McPeak had listened to this onslaught
in sullen silence, but at the mention of the
money he made a wild rush for the back
room with such a look of ferocity that
Mint arose and, keeping one eye on him,
slowly backed to the door.

In a flash he had unlocked and slammed
open the treasure house, only to find the
money gone!

With an oath the man turned and faced
Mrs. Julep.

" What has she done wi' my money? " he
shouted, shaking his fist in her face; " no
more o' yer domned blabbin', but tell me
thot."

He looked so fierce that for the first
time in her life Mint Julep cowed perceptibly, but it was only for a moment; then

"Your wife has lost every cent of that money"

she said pluckily, her hand on the door knob:

"Your wife has lost every cent of that money. It was jest as much hers as it was yours, and more — and she's sufferin' from the loss of it more'n you, for she's thinkin' o' someone else, but you're only thinkin' of yourself, and you deserve to lose more than that, fer you don't deserve a good wife. You're a brute!"

Mint opened the door and stepped out quickly, when an idea flashed into her head, and although her heart was beating wildly, she popped her head inside again.

"Your wife was so heart-broke this mornin' she said she hed a mind ter throw herself in the river, and yer better go down there and see if yer can't git her back for the sake o' takin' that miserable three hundred dollars outer her bones."

Then Mrs. Julep gathered herself together and marched off with head erect.

She hurried along to her own cottage, and on opening the door found Mrs. Mc-Peak on the verge of collapse.

"I guess after all we won't hev our company ter tea, Mrs. McPeak. Scotty's onlike my William in lots o' ways, but let me tell you one thing — you don't go near him, nor leave this house till he comes here and begs yer."

For answer the little woman buried her face in her gingham apron, crying as if her heart would break.

When McPeak was alone he flung himself into a chair and tried to think. The money was gone! Lost! Yes, that woman had just said "Your wife has lost every cent of that money." But how? He clenched his fists in impotent rage and gave himself up to every bitter, angry passion.

"How could Jennie have lost all that money? I'll wager thot bladgin' woman had some hand in it," said McPeak, as he arose and paced back and forth in the little room.

For a long time bitter anger and disappointment took possession of his being, his mind so filled with the loss of the money he could think of nothing else.

As the realization of his loss grew upon him there came thoughts, too, of his wife; what could Jennie have done with all that money? She had been so anxious to save, and was looking forward to owning a little home just as much as he, and still she had lost that money. It was almost incomprehensible and seemed as if he were in the grasp of a horrible nightmare.

Then visions of his wife grieving over the loss of it came to him, and his stern face softened. Other thoughts of her followed in quick succession.

It was the first time in their married life that Jennie had been out when he came home. It was a lonely, bleak place without her. He fell to wondering where she could be.

All at once Mrs. Julep's words came to him; she had spoken of the river. Merciful heaven! Why had he not listened to the woman!

He caught up his hat and rushed wildly out of the house, while his wife, weeping softly, watched him from behind Mrs. Julep's curtain.

The supper on the table " for the company " was untouched, but in the kitchen Mrs. Julep was busy giving the children " a bite," when some time later Mrs. Mc-Peak bounded into the room.

" He's back, he's back. Oh! Mrs. Julep, and he's comin' here.   What shall I say to Scotty!"

Mint had only time to thrust the woman into the kitchen and shut the door, when McPeak, after knocking, walked into the little entry way.

The woman was touched by the man's appearance; all trace of the sullen anger had disappeared from his face and a look of hopeless misery had settled there.

" I want ye to tell me aboot Jennie," he said quietly, though it was evident that the words cost him an effort.

" And I'll do it, Mr. McPeak, if you'll

promise me that you'll not say one word to her about that money."

" Dom the money — I want Jennie," he replied doggedly.

There was a faint squeal behind them and the next minute Jennie had thrown herself, weeping, into Scotty's arms.

" We'll have company to tea, after all," said Mint.

CHAPTER XII

WINTOP

DEER WILLIAM
    I have been watin for you to
    answer my last letter. You may
be sick. I hope so, as nothing else would
xcuse a man from writin to his wife an
famly.

I wrote and told you all about the trouble poor Mis McPeak was in an how I
had broke the news to Scotty that he had
lost his 300 dollars. Well I feel that I
done my part an done it well.

It was a good thing to remind that close-
fisted man that he had a wife that was
wuth more than his old money. Every
man who has got a good wife should know
that her price is above rubes, as the Good
Book says.

Well I guess that Scotty's heart is all rite an he thinks a lot of Jennie, cause I shall never forget the look on his face when he came into my entry to ask me about her.

I think that he had arrived to the conclushun that Jennie had committed a sewerside, for you remember I had told him she was goin to throw herself in the river. I can see him now as he stood there askin me to tell him, he looked like wot a preacher once called chaste in by sorrer.

Jennie says he has changed some since he lost the money. He dont give it to her now to save. He is puttin it in the saving banks himself.

Everybody I suppose has their favrit place to keep their money. As for me, I have allus favored my stockin, its handy, without bein too handy an youve got to go kind of private like to git at it an that makes yer careful.

Now William if you are sick your wife should know it before the world knows it.

Remember, I am almost anxshus about the stait of your helth.

Git Mr. Ogdin to write a line if you are laid up William to

Your lovin wife,
ARAMINTA JULEP

WINTOP

DEER WILLIAM

There seems to be no end to this terrible Beruba Plantation business. I am learnin of it at every side.

Ever sense I have come to Wintop to live I have allus traded at a little grocery store here that is kept by Mis Tobey. She is a widder woman with seven children. The oldest is a big girl and the youngest is a baby in arms.

Mis Tobey is a reel delicate woman an drags one foot jest a little, but she is full of pluck an has allus had a smilin face till lately.

I have noticed that lots of times when I go inter thet store to buy she seems ailin an kind of sad. She lives right back of the store and when you open the door it rings a bell in the kitchen an then she comes. Well, the other mornin I wated an wated an when she did come her eyes looked red from cryin — an tenny rate, I got a talkin with her bout the childern and sympathizin an long last says she —

Oh Mis Julep says she, Im in dredful trouble, says she. My husband left me this house an store free and clear. It made a livin for me an my childern, says she, but Ive done an orful thing. I invested some money I had, says she, hopin to get a fortune. An ajent came to me an talked and talked, an first I jest bought 2 shares, but it paid so well an he kept urgin me, so that at last I morgaged my childern's home, says she, and put the money into it, an it is not payin a cent, an the morgage is goin to be foreclosed. O, what shall I do, Mis Julep, an what is to become of my little childern?

Says I to her, says I Mis Tobey, if it aint askin too much, did you invest your money in the Great Beruba Plantation Company. Well, she jest bowed her head sobbin and sobbin.

I thot so, says I, an I done the same thing Mis Tobey an others have done the same. I had quite a talk with her an I told her not to feel so bad the Lord will provide, says I there will be a way to help you, you jest see if they dont. I said a whole lot to that poor worried woman to cheer her up a little an at last I went home.

O it is terrible sad William because you see she has all those childern to be looked after. It is a hard problem, an I am tryin to think of some way to help this poor woman.

This is all from your lovin wife.

MINT.

P. i. l.— I shall let you know how this all comes out.

WINTOP.

DEER WILLIAM —

The blow has fallen. It is too sad fer words, what I've got to write.

There was a drizzlin rain to-day an a cold east wind. I kep all the children in cept Jimmy — him I let out as he's tuff an hardy. Well Jimmy hadent been out long bfore he came runnin in Ma says he, Mis Tobey an all the children are turned out. The furnitoor is bein put on the street an they are all cryin.

Well William I grabbed my shawl an out I went, an I declare the sight would have made the stones melt. Two big husky fellows was emptyin that house into the wet street, while clingin round their mother was thet groop of weepin childern.

Mis Tobey looked like deth a holdin the baby.

Mis Tobey, says I, will you do me a favor, come right home with me, you an the young ones an then I'll tell you what it is.

She came with me meek enuff seems as if she had lost all sperrit, an I got em into my warm kitchen, an I told her to stay there while I went back a minute. Then me an Jimmy jest ran to where the furnitoor was bein put.

Says I to those husky villians says I if I was a man I'd learn you never to do anything but clean work long as you lived.

Then me an Jimmy started right in an we worked hard an carried that furnitoor, piece by piece into my cellar — beds an beddin cheers an tables, tin pans an all.

They are all damp of course but when a good dryin day comes along I shall try an dry evry one of them.

There was not sech a orful lot of stuff an Im a terrible fast worker when I get agoin William, an pretty soon we had it all in. The beddin I put upstairs. Then I went into the kitchen.

Says I, Mis Tobey, I've got evry bit of your furnitoor, says I, an youll stay right here for a spell. Wont it be nice, says I, for the childern. I love a house ful of childern, says I an a lot more. Well William she looked at me kinder mournful. She has great big brown eyes an there was dark circles under them.

Oh it is too much, Mis Julep says she, too much, an with that William she took sech a fit of coughin an her eyes looked so queer that I was scart. Her hand felt hot an I see she was a sick woman — an I put her right to bed lucky I have a foldin bed made up warm and comfitta-ble in my settin room.

Then I started in an I got up a feed for 12 childern, my five and her seven, an when they was stuffed full they all got a playin nice as could be. Jimmy an Mis Tobey's oldest girl, Bess, she's an orful pretty girl of 12 or so, got em all playin skule.

I xpect I'll have my hands full for awhile, but I'll write you a little later an tell you all about it.

Well, then I gave that darlin baby a nice warm bottle of milk, an got it sleep-in on a blanket in my cloes basket. I jest love babies, there is somethin about them that allus makes me want to git em close, seems sorter foolish when I have five, an Ham an Eg are only toddlers, but I jest cant help it, there never quite so dear to a mother seems to me as when they are jest little helpless babies.

This is all from your lovin,

MINT.

CHAPTER XIII

MINT SHOULDERS THE WIDOW'S TROUBLES

"TAKE this, Mis Tobey, and you'll feel better — the baby is fine — he's just had his bottle an' he's out there in his basket singing hisself to sleep, cute as can be."

Mint Julep was standing at the bedside cf the neighbor she had befriended, with a bowl of warm gruel in her hand, but the sick woman shook her head feebly.

"Thank you, dear Mrs. Julep, I hate to bother you, but really I don't feel like taking a thing this morning."

"A course you don't; sick folks never do, but they'd never git their strength back an' git well if they didn't take some nourishment; now jest set up for two minutes, there's a good woman, an' take this

91

little bit o' gruel, then you can have a nice sleep."

"It makes me feel so badly to know that I am here, a burden to you," began the woman as she raised herself in the bed.

"Tut, tut, Mis Tobey, I won't have any sech talk, you an' me are Christian women an' we ought to consider it a favor to help each other. Why good lands! I believe it was the Lord himself who sent me to Wintop to give you a hand jest as he sent the Samaritan of old to help that poor man who fell among the thieves.

"You an' me an' lots of other honest men an' women has fallen among the thieves of that Beruba Plantation Co.

"You was fleeced a little wuss than the rest of us, an' bein' sick, you ain't jest able to go on, but I'm a goin' to do the same as that other Christian did. I'm a goin' to do for you with my own hands an' you're a goin' to stay in the inn until you're able to go on with your journey, that's all there is to it." The sick wom-

an's lips trembled, and she took the prof-
fered gruel.

"God bless you, dear friend, you have
done a far greater thing than the Samaritan of old. I spoke to Dr. Roy," she
went on, "but he doesn't say much about
my going to the hospital, and so I am
hoping that it is because he knows I will
be about in a day or two."

"A course it wouldn't be wuth while
to go to the hospital for a short spell,"
said Mint, "you'll be up in no time. Why
I should be offul lonesome not to have
yer here, now that I've got used ter yer,
'taint a mite o' bother an' I jest love to
talk, if you jest rest an' save yer strength,
you'll be out of that bed in no time."

"Yes, I feel that I shall be up soon.
O, I must get out of this bed, Mis Julep,
think of those children and all I ought to
be doing for them."

"Well, the very best thing you can do
for 'em now is to stay right in bed to get
your strength back, then you an' me will
plan some good way to start all over again.

I'm orful good at plannin', Mis Tobey, things pop inter my head at jest the right moment. A woman of resources is wot the prefessor said of me onct an' I feel it's true. An' I allus look on the bright side. Why! If a mile o' freight cars came along loaded with trouble, an' dumped it all into my house, I'd find a way to git it out, sure as my name is Mint Julep."

" I believe you would," said Mrs. Tobey, and a smile suddenly appeared on the white lips that seemed to illumine her whole countenance. She started to say something, but a fit of coughing seized her and she closed her eyes and lay back exhausted. Mrs. Julep drew the curtains down and stole softly from the room, but she had not been in the kitchen five minutes when the woman called her.

" I'm a comin'," said Mint, reappearing at the bedside, " I've got a stew on, an' I jest went out to put in my rice. A stew is cheap an' fillin', orful good for children, an' not the least mite of bother

to make, now Mis Tobey, wot was yer
goin' ter say?"

"I was thinking, Mrs. Julep, that I
must do something very soon. Now I
know I'll never be strong enough to go
out working by the day, I couldn't do
washing and ironing and cleaning, but I
am a real good sewer. I love to sew."

"A course you do and it's the very
thing for you to do," said Mint, cheer-
fully. "Naow, if I do say it, Mis Tobey,
I jest hate to sew. I sew 'cause I've got
to, there aint nobody else to do it, but
there must be hundreds of women who
don't like sewing any more 'an me that
can afford to have somebody do it for 'em
and would be glad to pay a conscenshus
woman like you good wages. Yes, I
think plain sewin' would be jest the
thing."

"But Oh Mrs. Julep, perhaps I would-
n't get work all the time."

"Perhaps you wouldn't, 'taint likely
you will, but you can have a little store,
or somethin' beside the sewin' an' you've

got Bess to give you a hand with the children, an' my stars, you'll be jest as snug as a bug, an' I'll go an' give you a hand at the spring cleanin'. Then mebbe you could git a roomer or two. George is ten and a smart boy, he can earn a dollar a week, I'll bet a hoss. Why good land o' livin', when you git out o' that bed, an' me an' you put our heads together, they'll be sech schemes to make money as would make Mr. Vanderbilt set up an' take notice an' learn somethin' to his advantage. I'd only been in the city workin' for the prefessor three months when, I declare, in that time a dozen schemes to make a livin' came into my head. I 'member one day, Mr. Graves, wot had a office over the prefessor's, came in. He was the prefessor's wife's cousin, a reel nice man, a bachelor, allus jokin', an' this day he came into the prefessor's in a rush. ' I've got a train to catch,' says he, ' ain't got time to go to the tailor's and here's the sleeve of my coat all ripped.' I spoke up, says I, ' it won't take

me two minutes to mend that.' An' I got
my needle quick an' set to work. 'You're
a jewel, Araminta,' says he, 'an' wouldn't
it be nice if a feller like me had someone
to sew on buttons an' do the mendin','says
he. 'Why don't you git some one?' says
I. 'No one would have me,' says he, 'now
would they?' 'I wouldn't,' says I, 'if this
is a proposal, an' you wouldn't if you
knew a thing or two 'bout me.' Well, he
rolled his eyes like a playactor. 'Great
heavings,' says he, 'Araminta, is it possible you have a past?' 'Five,' says I, 'the
oldest is ten an' the youngest jest walkin'.'
Well, Mis Tobey, I thot that feller would
die a laffin, but I tell you wot it is the thot
came to me then an' there, that a woman
handy with her needle could git mendin',
an' pressin', an' fixin' for busy people in
those big buildings most any time."

"What a good plan that would be,"
cried Mrs. Tobey. "Oh, I feel that I will
be able to get on nicely if I only get well,"
and something of Mint Julep's faith got

into the soul of the sick woman and a look of hope came into her eyes that was good to see.

"Yes, there are ever so many chances in a big city," she continued, "but do you know that ever since I have been sick, I hate the city. I have wished many times that I was back in the country, and I have jest longed for the sight of green fields and apple blossoms."

"Well, that's a perfectly natral feelin'. When one is away from home an' ailin', it's nice to live in God's country where good things are free as air, an' there ain't no sign to keep off the grass, but I never surmised you was from the country. I allus kind o' put you down for a native of Wintop."

"No indeed, I lived most of my life in a little town in northern Vermont. I taught school up there, years ago. John was a teacher too, but he always had big ideas of going to the city and getting into business. He did real well too, when he came to Wintop, and Oh, to think of what

I have done with John's hard earn-
ings."

"There, there. Don't you begin a fret-
tin' 'bout it. It'll all come out right jest
see if it don't. You'll do well again,
p'r'aps better than you ever did in your
life; mistakes are made by everybody, they
come jest to make us a bit wiser for the
next, and a bit kinder to the feller that's
bound to make 'em. You'll be all right,
Mis Tobey. Why, one of these days
you'll be takin' a trip to your old home,
jest to see the folks for a nice visit."

"There isn't one of my folks left, Mrs.
Julep, and John hadn't a relative in the
world, but I'd like to see the place again.
It was very beautiful, and now that the
Spring days are coming, it makes me
think of the stretches of green country up
there and the smell of apple blossoms."

"Well, Mis Tobey, you jest get rested
an' well, an' everything is comin' out all
right. I feel it, and now I want you
should git a little sleep if you can. Molly
Burt said she was goin' to read to you

when she got home to-day, an' that will
be reel nice, for her voice is low an' soothin'
an' she's as cheerful to hev round as a
sunbeam in a empty garret."

CHAPTER XIV

THE LORD GIVETH AND THE LORD TAKETH AWAY

DEER WILLIAM,—
Miss Tobey had been sick in
Thanatopsis jest a week. The
doctor came evry day an at the last he
shuck his head an told me she could not
live. It was on a Friday night, William,
an all the children were in bed. He said
it jest outside in the entry but the ears of
the sick are sometimes terrible sharp an
she heard him, an when I went in there
was a reel peaceful look in her face as
she turned her big brown eyes on me.
It surprised me, cause all the week she
was most ravin sayin as how she must
git well, she must git up an work for her
childern. I had all I could do lots of
times to keep her in bed, a coaxin an

101

pleadin with her to save her strength, till
she got well, when she could do a lot
more. O, I had to say a whole lot to
keep her easy. Well, when the doctor had
gone I went in an she smiles reel cam an
peaceful like.

Dear friend, says she, I heard wot the
doctor said an I'm happy. I am ready to
go now. I had a dream this afternoon,
says she, an ever sense I have felt diffrent
about evrything. At first it was terrible
to be here sick an helpless and to think
of all I ought to be doin for my children.
Why this very afternoon, dear Mrs. Julep,
when you left me I was going over in my
mind all about planning to start again,
I guess I got excited. I tried so desperate to get out of bed, well, I got half
way out an then I fell back exhausted
and I cried from rage and disappintment. .
But the effort to get out of the bed made
me so tired that I fell into a sort of a
sleep. An then came the dream. It was
all green fields, an apple blossoms, an I
was walking through them happy and

smiling as a young girl and John (dear
John, he's only been dead a year) he
worked so hard for that house that he
was bent an gray before he went, but
in the dream he was not bent nor gray
nor worried, he was smiling and straight,
and seemed to be just waiting for me.
He was standing near a tree all blossoms,
and I kept walking toward him, nearer an
nearer till all at once I heard the baby
cry and I stopped. I cant come, John,
said I, the baby needs me. John never
said a word, he just looked over his head
and smiled at something and I looked an
saw a woman. Dear friend, it was like a
picture I saw once of the blessed Mother
of God. She had a little child in her arms
and floating all around her were butiful
children. Oh, I said, will you take care
of my baby, and all my little ones, and
at that she just smiled. It was like
heaven so peaceful and calm and holy;
but a great load was suddenly lifted from
my heart. I had no more doubts nor
longings, no more fears for my babies.

I wanted to go and I'm going. Oh, dear Mrs. Julep, you have been so kind to me and my little ones that God will bless you and if there is such a thing, says she, that I can help you when I am over there, I'll do it, dear friend, says she. An now let me see baby onct before I go to John, says she.

I went out quiet, William, an I brot in the baby. He is a dear little fellow, an he was sound asleep, but do you know that it seemed almost as if he knew what I wanted. He opened his eyes an put up his little chubby hands, an I took him up close to my heart. I love him already as if he was my own, an I brought him in, an laid his little cheek next to hers. Oh, William, I can never forget the look that came into her eyes.

" My little baby," says she, over an over. " My little, little baby." Then she kept lookin as if somethin was right over the foot of the bed an I took the baby gently away an went out an cuddled him up in the kitchen again, an went back an there

was Bess, the oldest girl, standin at the
door in her night gown.

"O, Mis Julep," says she, " I couldent
go to sleep for thinkin of mother. Is she
better?"

I couldent speak, William, seemed as if
I would choke if I did. I jest motioned
to the bed an Bess went over an stood
at the side. Her mother knew her an
smiled.

The dyin woman's lips were movin in
prayer, but all the time she kept lookin
hard at Bess.

I leaned over an I heard her say in
broken words, "Keep her, dear God,
Jesus, my Savior."

These were her last words. Her breath
came shorter an shorter, an her life went
out jest like a candle.

Bess threw herself across the foot of
the bed an sobbed as if her heart would
break. I put my hands together, William, an prayed as well as I knew how,
an I am still prayin whenever I think
of that pure spirit that tried an suffered

an did so much for her children. O,
dear God of pity an love, look down on
her little ones an show me the way to do
what is best for each an all of them.

MINT JULEP.

CHAPTER XV

DEER WILLIAM,—
The funeral is over. Thanks to Molly Burt, poor Mis Tobey was laid beside her husband.

I had been in kind of hard straits for money, as the expenses was a good deal. I pawned the lamp that the prefessor gave us for a weddin present, an I sold all my hens but five, then Molly Burt did the rest an helped me out. She could not do as much as she would have liked cause, you see her money is all tied up some way, but she is the soul of generosity an all I can say is I could have done nothin without her. Well, now I have got Mis Toby's belongins to settle about.

The furnitoor I am a goin' to dust an clean, an have an auction right on my front lawn. There's lots o useful things an the money is needed orful bad.

The children we shall decide about later. I spoke to Mis McPeak about takin one.

There's a little girl, named Jennie. She's orful cute, all curls an dimples, an Mis McPeak is jest crazy to adopt her but she's afraid that Scotty won't let her. I says to her, dont ask him at all, jest take her, says I.

Mis McPeak says, she dassent do that. I never see a woman that stands in sech fear of what her husband will do or say, but she says if she goes kinder on the quiet about it, praps she can take her. At any rate I send Jennie over there evry day and it would do you good to see Mis McPeak curlin her hair an fixin her up pretty. The little thing was kind of shy of McPeak at first, but now she runs an opens the door when she sees him, cryin out, Totty tomin, Totty tomin. Well, it kinder tickles McPeak, an the other night when she was sittin up at the table with them she fell fast asleep

over her bowl of bread an milk, an when
Mis McPeak got up an offered to carry
her home to me, Scotty spoke up an says
bide a wee, says he, Miss Julep has her
hands full.   Let her stay the night, said
McPeak.   Jennie said she was all of a
tremble with jest joy.   She had a little
baby onct many years ago, but she died
an I can see that Jennie McPeak's heart
is jest achin for that little motherless tot.
O it would be so nice if they would adopt
it.

McPeak is a stiddy, hard workin man,
gittin good wages an more than that they
are terrible thrifty, what with her roomers
an all, Jennie saves a lot of money, little
Jennie Tobey would have a good home an
Christian parents.   O, I am jest hopin an
prayin that this may be.

MINT JULEP.

CHAPTER XVI

" A NOVEL PLAN FOR DISPOSING OF BABIES "

DEER WILLIAM,—
Sech a wonderful thing has happened. A novel plan for disposin of babies is wot Molly Burt called it. Well, me an Molly Burt put our heads together to see what we could do with all those children. First of all, I must tell you that the McPeaks have legally adopted little Jennie Tobey, they are goin to call her Tobey McPeak because as McPeak said she had a good father an mother an ought to be reminded of it some way. McPeak is a wise man an just gruff at times an not much for nonsense an he's orful close but for all that the more I see of him the better I like him. Well, Molly Burt is goin to take Bess

Tobey, but she wants me to keep Bess until Molly herself is 21. She loves Bess, she says she never had a sister and always longed for one. She just loves that baby too. She said she wished she could smuggle him along too, but bless you young gals don't know nothin bout babies. One day when Molly was holdin of him, same as if he was a glass vase an might break, he started to holla an I thought I'd die a laffin',—

"Oh, Mis Julep, quick, take him quick, please take him," says Molly, " I think he is goin to choke."

Well, Bess and Jennie were provided for but they was five more, an one night when we was talkin it over an sayin' as how there must be lots of folks in the world that could love an take care of such nice children, I had a insperration. I told it to Molly an she went a purpose an told it next day to Mr. Jeremiah Storey, and a few days after, this notice was put in a big newspaper.

Wanted. Any honest, Christian woman
of means who likes children and has none,
will learn of something to her advantage
by calling at Thanatopsis Cottage, Grass-
hopper Lane, Wintop, Mass., on next
Tuesday afternoon at 3 o'clock.

We put the word " Wanted " in orful
big letters. Mr. Jeremiah said the ladies
were always wanting something, and that
word would catch their eye.

Well William Julep such a time as we
had. It was like a show, and best of all
it brought me my old friend, but wait,
I'll git to that.

In the mornin the hull tribe of kids
were playin in the dirt on my back steps
makin mud pies, nice as could be. I
guess that more dirt got into those children than into my steps, but that never
bothers me, some wise man said onct, you
cant raise chickens or children without
dirt, an I believe it. I keep mine warm
an dry, feed em just as well as I can,
lots of milk an eggs an broth, then I

let em play in dirt from Monday mornin
till Sateday night, when they are put in
the tub an scrubbed individule & Collective,
an I dont believe their is any healthier
childern in the state than mine. Well, I
had dinner early, an then I scrubbed an
scoured them children inside an out, an
made them look just as sweet an fresh
as I could. I dont know what I would
have done but for that sweet girl Molly
Burt a helpin me, an I set the children up
in a row in my settin room, and pretty soon
the bell rings an I went to the door and
William there stood my old friend, Bella
Ball, in a sweepin silk an parasol to
match, a hat big as a canopy an sech
hair. She looked perfectly bewtiful.
Well we jest hugged an kissed each
other. I allus did like Bella an the
strange part of it all was she never knew
I was Mis Julep. You see she came to
Farnham on a visit when the twins was
born an named em an after that we
kinder lost track of each other, but I told
you onct that she did not marry a Farn-

ham boy.   She married Henery Ball, who
came onct to Farnham on his summer va-
cation, an tenny rate it seems he is in
the soap grease business in Chelsea, an
they own their own home an are reel well
off.   The only thing Bella lacks for in
this world she says is a family.   She
wanted one, an Henery Ball wanted one
orfully but they never had one and then
she sees that notice in the paper and she
gets intrusted right away and comes over
to Wintop, never xpectin to see her old
friend, Araminta Backup, that was fust
of all, Allum *later* an Mint Julep that *is*.

Well, sayse I, Bella, take your choice,
I'd rather you'd have one than most any
body, and I told her the whole sad story
of the Tobeys, but while I was a talkin
to Bella, the bell rang again and a lot
of women, some old, some young, some
sweet, an some sour was on the porch of
my house, an I welcomed them in an
when I gets them all inside we was so
crowded that some had to stand in the
entry way.

I stood on a little hassock in the middle of the room an talked to them in a reel business like way.

A course, says I, who ever wants to adopt one of these childern will have to have references an be willin for Mr. Jeremiah Storey, the lawyer, to look them up. Then I held up that darlin baby, Johnny Tobey.

Here, says I, is a sweet blue-eyed baby boy, healthy an good natured. Who would like the dearest thing under Heaven, says I, jest for the keepin, dont all speak at onct, come rite up.

Well William you would think they was all struck dumb, no one moved an that made me mad.

Praps, says I, some of you has a puff poodle at hum, that you wash an sun an stuff an take out for a airin, he'll swell up an bust some day an that will be the end of him, but here, says I, is a little human soul that God made for love. There is good in evry human born into this world but its got to be developed some an brought out an nothin will bring it out like jest love. Now there is no knowin wot that little baby may become but you wont git Johnny Tobey not one of yer I will keep him myself.

Well with that Bella comes up an whispers, O, Araminta, says she, I want him, I would just love to have him, but I was thinkin I would like to have Henery here. And I want the little girl with the red curls, says Bella, (thats little Margaret Toby) keep em both Araminta, an I'm goin straight out an tellephune for Henery to come right over here.

Well I was orful pleased at that and then a reel sweet faced woman dressed in black came up an said she would like to talk with little Freddie. He is a handsome little chap jest 4 an I told her to take him out in my back yard an show him the hens an she would git him talkin reel cute an natral, an Freddie put his little hand in hers an went with her nice as could be an bime by she came back her eyes all wet from weepin.

I had a dear little fellow once, says she,
jest like Freddie but I guess God wanted
him more than I did.   Theres a big room
at home jest filled with his pretty toys an
a lonesome shaggy dog that watches them
evry day.   I thot I never could do it, she
said, but there's a look about Freddie.   I'd
like to take him home with me an see how
the toys like him.   If the shaggy dog
thinks it is all right I guess may be it is.

I felt a lump in my throat all the time
she was talkin William.   It was jest as if I
had looked inside a little corner of a mother's heart an found it all bruised an achin
an longin.   She slipped me a card with
her name and address on it.   She's a Mrs.
Davis an a reel lady an best of all Mr.
Jeremiah knows all about her.   He sent
her to us.   I feel so happy.   What a
great thing for that little child if he gits
a mother an home like this an as for that
sweet woman who knows but what that lit
tle orphan boy may do much toward heal-
ing a poor broken heart.   Oh, I know
dear Mis Tobey is pleased to-day an I

thank the dear God for this favor.

Dr. Roy, who attended Mis Tobey wants the boy. He is goin to take George Tobey, who is ten an educate him an George can do little chores for he's a big strong boy.

Well then, there was only little Bud left. She is a little gal of 7, with a face like an angel but she's lame, and nobody wanted the little lame chicken. I would not put her up to talk about, William, I jest couldent. I called her to me across the room so thet they would all see she was lame, an then I put my arm around her and I said I guess I cant let Bud go, I want her myself. Nobody offered to take Bud so I hugged her close. I only have one little gal, Bud, says I, an she's a fly-away, an rough as a boy. I want you to be my little gal too, and see if Mamie wont git to be sweet an gentle like you. Well William she jest hid her face in my dress. Oh, Mis Julep, says she, I'd like to stay here with you. And here she stays William long as the dear Lords wants I should keep her. She'll git what mine git an better if I can do it, an when the day comes that I shall have to render a account of my stewardship I shall say I did the best I knew how.

This is the whole story from
Your lovin wife,
ARAMINTA JULEP.

CHAPTER XVII

Lost, a Duc and Old Curiosity Shop

DEER WILLIAM:
Every thing is goin along reel nice here. The children are well an Molly Burt seems happy an contented now.

Last night I was sewing, all the children 'cept Bess an Jimmy was in bed. Bess was helpin me, she's orful handy with her needle, an that oldest boy of ourn was readin.

He's pesessed lately to read. I sent him up stairs one day to clean up his room, an after waitin an waitin for him to git through an come down, I tip-toed up stairs to see what was keepin him so long.

Well I never made a sound an I opened the door quick an peeked in, an there was

Jimmy on his stummick with a book under
his nose.

I thot at fust he was eatin it, an I dont
know as it would have surprised me much
if he was, for boys eat most any old thing,
an my Jimmy has a stummick that could
digest hoss nails.   Talk about devourin a
book, thats jest wot Jimmy was doin.

I let a offul loud coff, that made Jimmy
jump.   He was terrible supprised at seein me,—Wots it about, Jimmy says I, an
is it as good as all that.

Mother says Jimmy, its great, they have
got the slooth into a hut an theres three
hundred Injuns guardin it, but he sees a
way out.

Says I you had best see a way out of
here to do your chores quick Jimmy, or
I'll be wuss nor those three hundred Injuns, says I.

I told Molly Burt about it, an she laffed
an said he was jest at the age where his
taste for readin is being formed.

She's offul kind, she had a reel nice talk

with Jimmy an she let him take a book, an she says now Jimmy, I want you to read it an tell me honestly how you like it. An Jimmy did, an the very next day he says dont yer read it Miss Burt, says he, theres nothin doin.

Well Molly laffed an laffed. Then she let him take another. Its about the Crusaders, she told him a lot about them, an Jimmy liked it reel well, an when he finished it she got him another.

Well wot I started to say at the beginnin of this letter was that the night that Bess an I was sewin, an Jimmy readin, Molly Burt came in an sot an we got talkin about books. Molly jest loves to read.

I told her that Bella Ball was jest plumb crazy, when we was gals, about readin books. Bella was allus coaxin me to read books that she did, but I never could git intrusted in 'em. They was allus too long gittin married to suit me.

But that Bella Ball, how she would weep over them gals in the story books. I member onct Bella jest begged me to read a book that had set her weepin for a week.

The name of it was—Lost—a Duc—or Weddin the Wrong Man. Well Bella cried a bucketful over that book, an at last I give in to her pleadin an read it, an I never shed one weep over it. I was mad clean through over that book, thats what I was. Says I to Bella taint strange says I that the Lady Gwendolin married the wrong man says I, wot surprises me is that a female like her could git any man rite or wrong to marry her.

O, Araminta, says Bella, have you no sole. I have says I, two of them, an I'd take 'em both, fust one an then the other, an boot the Duc De-Swamp-Flees outer Farnham.

More'n that says I, I'd take the Lady Gwendolin an put her into a asslum for the feeble minded, says I.

That was the only book I ever read all through, and I didnt quite finish that but Bella told me stories she had read an I will say some of them warnt half bad.

Orful romancin gal was Bella. I'll

never forgit one Hollow Eve night, Bella
an me went to a barn dance.

We ducked for apples an played games,
an we had a reel good time an that night
on the way home, me an Bella agreed to go
upstairs backward an git inter bed backward an do a lot of things upside down
to see if we would dream of our future
husbend.

Well I did dream that night. I have
never dreamt much in my life, an when I
do, its perfeckly ridicalus. That night I
was chasin' naked savages all over Farnham. Perfeck nightmare thats what it
was, an no wonder, for Bella an me had et
a whole mince pie fore we went to bed.

Well the very next day Bella ran in to
me breathless, O Araminta says she, sech a
dream as I had says she, an she acktually
groned,—was it your future husband says
I, I'm not sure says Bella scairt like, I
dreamt of a man but O Araminta says
she, he looked like the devil, orful dark
with a mustarch that pointed upwards.

Bella says I, if you marry one of them

furriners, we part friendship forever says
I. Well I told all this to Molly an we
had sech a good time laffin about books, an
bime-by Molly took out a book, this is one
of my favorites says she; its so good an it
has give me so much pleasure that I'd like
to share it with the whole world says she.

Share it with us Molly, says I, tell us
about it, or whats better still says I, read
a little, that is if you dont mind.

I'd love to says Molly an I'm sure you
will enjoy it.

Well William, Molly has a voice sweet
an low an clear as a bell,—its a reel pleasure to lissen to her readin, it was as if you
was rite there with the pusson in the book
an seein every thing yourself. An the
book was diffrent from anything I ever
heard tell of, or anything Bella Ball ever
read.

The name of the book was the Old Curiosity Shop. Even Jimmy an Bess got interested in a dear little creature that they
called Little Nell, an the way she follered
her old grandpa round, a watchin of him,

an guardin him an tryin to protect him, an she nothin but a child herself.

Well William it was wonderful and kinder sad, there was other karacters in that book that was reel funny an made us all laff.

One was a little crooked man named Danel Quilp thet I think was pesessed of seven evil sperrits, he was a queer chap, an O William Danel was missin fer a few days an some men came to git a description of him from his mother in law an I'll never forgit it, for Danel came in an was hidin behind the door an heard every word his mother in law said to those men about him. William Julep I never laffed so much in my life, I laffed so hard that Molly had to stop an laff too.

I never knew they had sech nateral goins on in books as was here. Some how they are so reel, that you never think of 'em as bein in books, seem as if they was old friends an might walk in any minnit an set awhile.

Well we made Molly promise that she

would read some every night till the story
was finished, an Molly was jest ticklled
to do so.   She told us about some other
books by the same man as wrote Little
Nell, Molly says they are the best books
ever written an she wants Bess an Jimmy
to read every one of them.

She knows a heep about books an has
wot the perfesser would call a highly cul-
tered mind.   Molly says the greatest one
of all the books this man rote, is called
David Copperfield, an she is goin ter start
it fer me by readin it aloud an then she
says I'll finish it myself.

Well William its offul nice an cosy here
an I wish you was at home to enjoy it
all.   It would make yer heart glad to see
Molly an Bess, with their arms around
each other, jest like two lovin sisters.

Molly is so sweet an lady like that I
cant help thinkin every time I see 'em together, if Bess is like that pure, sweet gal,
her dear mother in Heaven must be smilin
an happy.

YOUR LOVIN MINT.

CHAPTER XVIII

WILLIAM'S PAR AND MAR ARRIVE

DEARIST WILLIAM

Sech a surprise as I have fer you, but yisterday I was peelin my pertatoes fer dinner when Ham an Eg walked inter the kitchin, leadin a nice appearin couple, gent an lady. The gent put down his carpet bag on the floor an says to me reel smilin,— misses William Julep low me to introdooce mister an misses Tom Julep of Little Acres.

Yes William as I live, your par an mar; fust time they had ben away in 20 year. An they never knew you was out in the Rockies, which was wrong of you William never to have writ a line to your folks.

You orter pray William to overcome thet terrible failin of yourn of not talkin or writin — if you did you would never go away from home an not write a line

128

to the best friends a man can ever own this
side of heaven.

Well William there was your par an
mar a standin there, an Jimmy an Mamie
an Tommy an Ham an Eg an Bess an
Bud a standin there waitin for devilope-
ments an I felt that pleesed I jumped up
an I grabbed the childern an I said welcome, welcome, welcome to Thanatopsis an
then an there we jest played ring around
arosy, with par an mar an the carpet bag
in the middle.   Your par laffed an laffed,
he enjoyed it I could see, but your mar
got nervous when Ham an Eg fit like imps
on the bag, to see who was goin to open it.

Well here they be an here I'm agoin
to make them stay fer a spell an I want
you should write them a nice letter an
give them word there welcome to Thanatopsis.— I have jest had an idee, I will
write the letter cause you cant, William,
an inclose it in this one then you send it
direck to your folks from the Rockies an
this will pleese your lovin wife

MINT JULEP.

P. I. L.

I should talk William if I hed to talk to myself, an if you done sech a thing I dont know thet you could be talkin to a better man.

I wish you was comin home William, we are all jest pinein to see you.

Mint.

Wintop.

My Deer Husbend

I now take pen in hand to remind you of the felicitudes of life. I hed a telagraph today from Farnham thet contained sad news. William you'd never guess what was in thet telagraph — life is made up of losses an crosses an when they come we got to take them.

You an me cant go slidin down the hill of life without gettin some bumps — William Julep we've jest hed a bump.

You an me is no diffrent from the rest of creation — I onct heard Mister Godwin say thet life is how we take it an I know now thet he meens how we take losses an crosses.

William you must make up your mind
to beer up like a man, an dont forgit thet
whot ever happens you've got your Mint
Julep an the childern, but if the Good
Lord should see fit in his all wiseness to
call me to my reward I'll go,— not thet
I expect much William but I do expect
more than Luther Day thet uster sell coal
in Farnham an was up before the orthor-
ities more than onct fer givin short weight.

When Luther died I'll never forgit
what mister Godwin said, says he, our
brother has gone to his reward says he,—
well I kept a thinkin of them words William — Gone to his reward says I, an he
sold coal an sold it short. The ways of
Providence is far seein William, Luther
was given his chanct in this world to see
what he'd do with coal — He was short —
I dont beleive he'll ever be short on coal in
the next.

But as I was sayin William if I should
pass to my reward, I wouldent expect you
to mope around here without a wife, you
need a woman more than the avrage Wil-

liam — You are one of them critters what takes what ever is handy but you dont never reech out,— you need a wife to reech out fer you.

I have been reechin out all my life fer some one an when I git on the other side I expect I'll have to reech out an help some one over.

I dont beleeve I'd ever leeve the selecshen of a female to you William, I should want to see her an git her broken in before I went.

I've set my heart on it thet Tommy should be a moosichen as you know, an Jimmy somethin ekally as good. I hev changed my mind about Jimmys bein a orrater. He does hate to hear hisself talk an orraters dont hev thet failin'. A good medisin docter wouldent be bad fer Jimmy,— half the folks you meet are allus ailin an the other half thinks they have ailins so them medisin fellers git all they want to do.

An they dont hev to talk much either —

most of them jest set up an look wise an send a bill. Pa says a hoss-doctor aint bad neither.

I expect Mamie will hustle all her life same as me. She's jest like me ceptin fer the tack, which she cant seem to git in her.

Regardin the twins well Ham an Eg is most too young to think of settin them up in bisness, but I shouldent be surprised if they'd turn out painters or the like for twas only yisterday thet they made a border of little round holes on the kitchin wall with nuthin but there naked fists an molasses, t'warnt tidy as your mar said, but as I said it was reel cute an showed a desinein mind.

But Hirams wife is dead an gone William (Peggy Barnes that was) an a good woman she was too though she was pessessed to git her beans too salty, an she died of a Tuesday an will be berried of a Friday. Par an Mar will mind the childern while I go to Farnham, poor Hiram I do

pitty him alone.   It isent good fer man
to live alone William, the Good Book says
so.

Your sorrowin an greevin

ARAMINTA JULEP.

P. I. L.

It hes jest come to me that it is fittin
you should write a letter to Hiram consolin
him in this our of his bereevement.

I dont dast trust you to do it, so I shall
hev to write it inclose it with this an you
send it direck from the Rockies to

Mister Hiram Cuckoo Backup
Farnham.

CHAPTER XIX

MOVING THE HENS TO CHELSEA

DEER WILLIAM,
There are some folks in this world thet may have their use, but its orful hard for others to figger out jest what 'tis.

There's a cantankerous single man, wot has a impedelment in his speech, roomin' at McPeaks. His name is Rorer, Benjamin Rorer. The McPeaks don't care much about him, cause he's allus behind in his rent. Well William it seems he has made objections to my hens — he said the rooster crowed too loud an too early, an he was loosin his sleep, an a whole lot more. Did you ever hear of anything so ridicalous.

I have allus felt proud of Dick — He's better than any alarm clock in the town,

135

cause you dont never have to wind him
up,— he's sot for four o'clock for life.

Well tenny rate, I got word from the
authortees last week that I must part with
my hens. I never was so surprised in
my life. I felt bad an Mrs. McPeak felt
bad cause I often give her a fresh egg.

Your Par was mad as a hornet about
it, an when the Board o Health man came
round next day, Par said a whole lot to
him.— Why! says Par wots a few hens —
I was goin ter buy a caf for Tommy there,
an ding me ef I dont. You better not,
says the health man, this aint the country,
you know, an you'll git inter all sorts of
trouble. Well after he went away Par
jest raved — not git a calf if I want one,
says Par.—

" Things has come to the purtiest pass
the world has ever sawn, ef an old duff
cant let a caf, chaw grass on his own front
lawn! "

But to git to the hens — Scotty
McPeak who is terrible shrude an long
hedded, told me to send the hens away

for awhile an lay low, an then bime-by
bring 'em back. He xplained as how I
could worry out this Rorer till he quit his
complaints.

Well I dident know jest what to do
about sendin 'em away for awhile, 'taint
as tho you could send five hens an a rooster
visitin',— not but what they'd pay their
way.

However I hated to part with my hens,
an at last I thot of a scheme.   There was
Bella Ball in Chelsea.— Bella was from
Farnham, I argeyed, an as sech was allus
used to hens, an Farnham folks was allus
accommodatin', moreover Bella had borrowed off me as a gal, every thing I
owned 'cept my skin; why I'll never forgit onct she borrowed my stays to wear
to a huskin'; I had to fill out some way
so I got some stiff paper an made a sort
of emergency stays that answered the
purpose all right as far as the looks went,
but every time I danced that paper made
an orful noise, an onct when Hicks Bosworth was swingin' he says rite out —

"I allus thot you was thin, Mint, but I never heerd yer bones rattle before."

Bella was balancin' us on the opposite corner, an she said she thot she'd die a laffin.

But to git to the hens agin, I felt that Bella would help me out, an besides I wanted to see the Tobey children, Johnny an Margaret, so I'd kill two birds with one stun, git the hens over outer harms way, an pay a visit all to onct.

Them health men gave us three days to git rid of the hens, an on the third mornin' I put on my black dress an my cashmere shawl, an we started, me an Par an Jimmy.

Par an Jimmy had baskets with two hens in each, but we couldent raise another basket nowhere, so I tuck Dick right under one arm, an the brown pullet under the other.

I knew my shawl would hide 'em so that no one in the car would be a bit the wiser.

Well Par had a little argyment with

the cornducter when we was gettin on,
'bout the baskits, but Par assured him that
they was well behaved poultry, an wouldent cause no annoyance, but he insisted
on Pa's leavin the baskits outside; so tenny
rate on we got, an Jimmy got right in the
farthest corner, then Par, an then me.

Now I dont never look much at folks
in a car, 'taint perlite, but direct oppsite
sat two Hebrew gents, an If I do say
it one of them was terrible cross-eyed.
They was talkin' hard at each other in
a furrin tongue, seemed like they was
havin a seerius argyment, an all the time
their hands was agoin backard an forrard,
then they'd git their faces orful close,
noses most touchin' an then they'd back
out agin. Well I got so intrusted watchin' them two, I never noticed right next
to 'em sot a laborin' man; he had on blue
jeans stuffed inter his boots all spattered
with white stuff, looked like he was a plas-
terer, an he wore a soft felt hat pulled
down over his eyes. He was sprawled
out dozin quiet an cam, till all to onct I

see him give a start an he sot right up
starin' at somethin' on me!

I looked down, an there was Dick pokin
his head out from under my shawl a little
way, an lookin right over at that man,
cute as could be. But I'll never forgit it,
all in a suddent, that man in the blue
jeans had riz a foot in the air, an was
makin hot for the rear door.

He staggered orful, squeelin *snakes!*
lemme go — leme go, — men hollered, an
a stout lady near the door fainted ded
away.

It was so dredful suddint, I forgot I
had a hen an rooster tucked under my
arms, an 'fore I knew it, Dick was chasin'
the brown hen through the car. Every
body had riz up an was sassin every one
else. Onct I see Dick light on the Hebrew gents Derby, an onct I see Par on
all fours tryin to git him.

Agin I see Dick slidin down the Hebrew's front, while that poor laborin' man
at the door, cried like a child.

Then a short haired lady with a man's

shirt boosom on, riz up an tried to hit
Dick with her umbrel; I couldent stand
fer that, I jest sassed her,— Says I he's
mine, I'll git him an dont you dast tech
him.

With that I grabbed my skirts up,
which made 'em all holler wuss, an then
an there, if I do say it William, for jest
two minutes Mint Julep ran amick
through that car.

I never heard so many profane lan-
guages in all my life, but when I gits
through I had Dick by the legs, while the
brown hen was restin' on the Hebrews'
front.

The other Hebrew was fannin' a stout
lady with a little card; he was reel kind
an he kept a sayin' to her, its nodding
lady, roosters do dem tings some dimes.
Nice of him, war'nt it.

A big fat man settin next to the short
haired lady, most had hystericks; he was
wipin' his face an shakin' tremenjus, an
tears was streamin' down his face, he was
so wrot up.   The whole circumstance was

puffectly orful while it lasted, an when I sot down pantin' I see strong men shakin' with fear.

The cornducter was furus, onct he shook his fist at me an was cussin like time; but then they stopped the car an the laborin' man was took off. A blond lady who was chewin gum, was tellin' every one they could'nt fool her, she said 'twas plain as day that man had the horrers.

Well when all was quiet agin an I had Dick an the hen under my arm, as every one knew I had a hen an rooster, I jest put them boldly outside my shawl to git the air an all to once Dick crowed rite out spunky as could be. Every body laffed fit to die, 'cept the lady wot had the short hair an a mans boosom; she shivered; I bet she jest despises to see a rooster. I have a orful lot of respect for Dick, he blows his trumpit the best he knows how, an he wants the whole world to hear it.

Well after I'd been settin' a while I

see the Hebrew gent wot caught the brown hen was lookin over reel pleasant, only as he was crosseyed I couldent tell whether it was at me or Dick or the brown hen; at last he leans way over an says to me —

How much you sell him for?

That's a hen says I, thinkin' he was lookin' at it.

Vell how much you sell him for, what you take for the two?

How's that says Par, scentin' a trade right away, want ter buy poltry mister, I have two baskits outside.

Well I dunno, how much for the bunch, says the Hebrew.

Then I spoke up,— Mister says I, they aint fer sale, I am jest takin' them to a friend fer a visit, says I.

So-o says he, an then he pulls out a little card an handed it to Par; if you change your mindt says he, let me know.

On the card it said in big letters writ nice and plain like this it said:

Israel Sink

Junk-

Blosson Court.

Well 't last we got to Bella's street
an that cornducter was sayin' terrible un-
compliment things 'bout us all the way
out; we did'nt take no notice but jest
walked right down to the house an rang
the bell, an who should come to the door
but Mary Banks. Old Si, wot kept the
hotel, his granddarter from Farnham.—
She's been helpin at Bella's for ever so
long.

And war'nt Bella delighted to see us.
Would she keep the hens, says I.

" You dear droll thing, says Bella, of
course I will, I'd do any thing for you
Mint.

Would Henery Ball object says I.

Never says she, he worships the groun
I walk on says she. An its no wonder

William, Bella was a pretty gal allus,
but now she's more, she's a reglar raving
beuty.

She tuk us all over her house, It is
grand. I never see anything like it in
her parlor; you have ter wind your way
in an out like a mazy with statoos an
pottery an brick-er-brack. A gold cupid
with wings out-spred was swingin' from
a hook in the middle of the ceilin, shootin'
darts. Par dodged, but got hit twict.
Par's tall yer know.

Says I, Bella your home is grand, an
you deserve it, you was allus a good warm
hearted gal, says she, it only lacked a
baby an now I've got two, thanks to you,
you dear Araminta, says she; my Henery is just silly over 'em says she, why he
left his factory this afternoon an has 'em
both out ridin' in his buggy.

Well I was ticklled to hear that. Then
she goes out to git us a cup of tea an
me an Mary Banks got ter talkin' old
times, till Bella called an ast her to go

an git me a crock of her red currants,
knowin' that I was allus partial to her
way of doin' them up.

Your Par was terrible imprest by the
house an by Bella, I could see that.

Aint Bella a handsome woman Par,
says I.

Yep, says Par, showy, but sound.
Ding me, says he, if I was twenty year
younger an Henery was plyin his trade
above, I'd go in myself, says Par. We
was still laffin when Bella come in and
told us to come out to the dinin' room.

My lands! sech a good bite as she had
got up fer us, 'twarn't only a lunch Bella
said, as they had six o'clock dinners; we
enjyed it I can tell yer, an we talked lots
over old times.

Bime-by Par and Jimmy went out in
the yard ter fix a place fer the hens an
Bella takes me up stairs to her room —

William Julep, a gold bed on my word
of honor! I was dumb at the site — Is
it wuth a fortune Bella says I, O no says
she, laffin. Then she showed me all her

julery an things an says she to me, Araminta Julep you an me are the same age, says she; well no one would ever know it says I, you look ten years younger than me.

'Course I do says she; you was a nice lookin gal Mint, you allus had fine eyes an was strait as an arrer, but you havent kept up says she. Now Araminta says she, fust of all you've got to wear your hair diffrent.

How can I says I, my hair is offul thin, I'm allus in a hurry an the quickest way I can git it up, the better, says I. I do go at it like I had a rake 'stead of a comb, says I.

It has fallen out by the bushel, an like the bad seed in the Bible, I have gathered 'em in bundles to burn.

All wrong says Bella,— you must brush it an you should have saved all your combins an had puffs made like mine.

Says I, Bella Ball, honor brite cross yer heart, is that yours, or the seven Sutherland Sisters.

Well she laffed an she says I'll tell you a secret, Mint, says she, an she opened a door an I see Switches of hair, all sizes a hangin'. She opens a draw an I see puffs, an curls an round hairy hay-lows, enough to stuff a pillow.

Mint says she, you've got to git hair; you owe it to yourself an you owe it to your husband to git some hair.

Now says she, Hair is my weak spot, every time I go to Boston, I buy hair, I simply cant help it, says she.

Now Mint says she, our hair is the same shade an I'm goin' to arrange a coffer on you. Then William she got me in front of her mirror, she twined ropy hair around my head, she put on a load o' puffs with hair pins, an hangin down a bunch o' curls; she called it a wata-fall or catract, I disremember. Then she stud off an kissed me, she's offul affectionet an coaxin in her ways, Bella is.

Now you must promise me that every afternoon of your life, you'll fix up your hair in glory; You look like a diffrent

"Mint" says she "you've got to git hair"

bein says Bella, an honest I felt that I did.

Now says she, you aint a goin ter wear any more bonnets.

The idea of a young woman like you tyin' on a bonnet; she tuk it up — No Bella says I, I bourt that bonnet to marry William Julep says I an it cost considrable, an I like it.

Well says Bella you can never tie strings over all that hair I put on yer, it would be ridicalus; if you must wear it, says Bella, let me loop up the strings inter cute little rosetts, an pin it on like a hat.

So we got a talkin about wimmen an wimmen's bewty an William I hev come to the conclusion that any woman born with a nose can be bewtiful.

In a big city William you can buy any thing; wimmen get eye-lashes an golden hair, a elegant shape an have their toe-nails bewtified. Bella Ball is the same, an yit not the same, but of this I am certain, if she was a widder tomorrer, which I hope she will never be while she has

Henery, she could git any moulten millionaire in America, an as for her ever goin abroad,— I dont dast think of it, for they say King Edward settin over there on England, is a reel nice gent wot likes the ladies xtremely well. Who knows William wot might happen. Kingdoms has been thrun away for wuss nor Bella. Bella is bewtiful William, she is most too bewtiful.

Well we spent an offul nice visit, an then we went.

Every body was lookin at me in the car. I felt as if I was carryin' a load of hay on my head, but your Par likes it. P. I. L.

We told Bella about the Gent wantin ter buy the poltry; she warnt surprised at it. She says as how a Hebrew jest loves to git hold of a live goose or any thing in that line.

Deer William,—

To-day was a very warm day an I hurried up an got my work done and was jest gittin ready to go down to the water with par an mar an the children when who walks into my front door but a man. I had my back to him as I was buttoning up Ham an I turns quick to see who it was an there stood Hiram Cuckoo Backup in his best black suit, yaller tie an lookin natral as life.

"Why, brother, I'm right glad to see you, but wot ever pessessed you to leave Farnham at this season of the year," says I.

"Business, Mint," says Hiram. "I had pretty important business in Boston an I thot I'd run in an see you."

"Will William seein as how he did'nt offer to tell me wot the business was I wouldent ask him but I was jest bilin with curiosity to know wot business made Hiram Cuckoo Backup come clear to Boston.

He agreed to stay over for a few days an he was reel nice to the childern, gav em all pennies, an then sot down on my front porch to cool off, but bime-by he got inter a dredful hot argyment with your par bout some man named William Jennings O'Brien. You know William that I told you onct how Hiram Cuckoo is quick tempered an has a slight impedalment in his speech. When he is cam you dont never notice it but when he git xcited its orful bad cause he has got a most peculeer habit of raisin his right leg, an his right arm to onct when the words stick an seem to most throttle him. Well Hiram got red in the face praising this O'Brien man but your par was dead sot again the gentleman an long last I got so dreadful nervous I ran down the street an bot some ice-cream to cool Hiram off. Hiram was allus quick tempered but I have sometimes thot it was kind of cruel to give him the name my par and mar gave him. A name like Hiram Cuckoo would make a phonographic machine stutter.

You see my par had a favrit brother named Hiram, who went to live in Cuckoo, Virginny. He named his fust born Hiram Cuckoo an my par just to please that brother away off named his own boy Hiram Cuckoo an poor Hiram got into lots of trouble on account of that name.

I remember onct when Hiram was off on one of his walkin tours he see a quarrel between two farmers that came to blows an tenny rate one sued the other an the case came to court and Hiram had to go as a witness an when he gits on the stand the lawyer feller says, whats yer whole name. Well of course poor Hiram was scart an kind a excited an he couldent say that name to save his life. The lawyer feller got mad an Hiram got madder an last Hiram med a dive outer the witness stand and hit him. He was fined for it.

Well, William, this is all from your lovin   MINT.

P. I. L.

I hev ben puzzlin my brains till they ake tryin to guess wot Hiram's business is. You know Hiram has a tidy fortune thanks to Peggy Barnes, an not a chick or child to leave it to.

CHAPTER XX

DEER WILLIAM

I am all through with keepin' hens. Sorry as I am to say it, I have come to the conclushon that Thanatopsis aint the most comfitable place to keep five hens an a rooster.

It was like this, you see Bella Ball kept my hens two weeks, an then Henery sent them back in a big wooden box, cosy as could be. They arrived in the afternoon an I put them in their old place in the back yard. Well the very next mornin Dick crowed as he never crowed before in his life an Benjamin Rorer came to the winder in his night shirt, an he threw boot-jacks an other things in my yard tryin to hit that poor Dick.

Me an Par heard the racket an we sassed

154

him an then Hiram got up an sassed him too.

Well bime-by after breakfast Par said he thot 'twas kind of foolish to be havin trouble all the time on account of the hens, seein as how Rorer had the law with him. You best git rid of them, says Par to me, but says I, I'll move away first, wot good would that do, says Par, there's a Rorer in every community says he,— well your Par is wise William an I respec his opinions, an I thot it over, he advisin me strong ter sell 'em.

You just say the word, Araminta, says Par, an I'll drop a post card to the Hebrew gentleman wot was so taken with Dick that day on the car, that he offered to buy the hull lot. Says I praps its all .fer the best Par, go ahead an write to him says I, an then an there Par sot down an wrote to the Hebrew gent, that he could buy five hens an a rooster most any time.

Now I was kinder sorry that Hiram Cuckoo should have happened to be visitin at the house jest when we was havin

the trouble, cause his temper gits to the
bilin pint on the slightest provocashun;
an all the time he was eatin his breakfast,
he was xpoundin his way to Par to git
even with Benjamin Rorer. Well he
was so powerful wrot up I see its about
time to say somethin to Hiram, so I spoke
up an I says to him,

Now look here, Hiram says I, you
mustent think no more about this affair,
this aint Farnham an folks are diffrent
here,— it aint Christian to be talkin of
gettin even, remember Hiram says I,
Vengence is mine, sayth the Lord. Let
you an me be charitable, Hiram, who
knows but this Benjamin Rorer may have
some secreet sorrer nawrin at his witals,
so that he cant stand a rooster crowin.
He is a lone man Hiram, an who knows
wot akes an longins may pesess his sole.
But taint no use, you might as well talk
to the habitants of a graveyard as ter try
to make a impression on my brother Hiram or git him to cool off his rath.

Well William that same afternoon sech

a thing happent as I'll never forgit long as I live.

The childern was all down to the water with your Mar, for wich I must say I was thankful, an Par an Hiram was havin it out on the front porch about Mr. O'Brien an free silver.

I was dustin in the parlor, when all at onct the two Hebrew gentlemen wot was on the car that day we went to Chelsea, walked rite into my front gate. They was reel nice an familiar to Par an he gave them a introduc to Hiram Cuckoo. You'd most think they was old friends, they shook so sosial like.

Well I stept out an said how do, an talked a little an bime-by we all went into my back yard to look at the hens.

Long last we came to terms, the price was paid, an then I told them to go into my parlor with Par to wait while me an Hiram started to git the hens ready for them.

We got Dick an the hens into the kitchen when I happent to think of the big box wot Henery Ball had sent 'em home in.

I sent Hiram down the cellar for it, an while he was gone I stept over to the winder, an who should be standin in my back yard but Benjamin Rorer an a strange gent.

Like a flash it came to me that it was the Health man for the hens, an I made a dive an grabbed up those hens, two at a time, an I ran an threw 'em into the parlor at Par an the Hebrew Gents. Them two strange men dident know what ter make of me doin sech a thing, they jumped an the hens made a orful fuss, cacklin an flyin, but I was reel excited, says I keep em out of sight,— hide em,— quick, the Health man is comin. Then I went out quick an shut the door.

It was kinder hard I know to shut three grown men, five hens an a offul stirrin rooster, in one little room, but it was a desprit case an had to be.

Well I got back into the kitchen jest as the door opened an that cantankerous

Rorer an the Health feller walked in, an trouble allus does come in a heep, William, for no sooner did they set foot in that kitchen, than my cellar door opened and Hiram Cuckoo sticks in his head, draggin the big box behind him.

But Glory! when he sees Rorer he lets that box go slam bang down the cellar stairs, an in he falls rite on his stummick, in his haste to git into that room; but he gits on his feet quick, w-w-w wot d-d-d-dy yer w-w- want h-h- here, says Hiram to Rorer, trying to stiddy hisself, an hold hisself in like.

Th-th- those d-d-d- dam hens, says Rorer.

O the pity of it William, that Hiram Cuckoo Backup did not know that Benjamin Rorer had a impedelment jest like hisself, but he did not.

D-d-d-d dont d-d-dare m-m-mock m-me you white l-l-livered —— the rest I will not write William, because it would be wrong. You are not a profan man, nor yit a heavy talker, enuff to say that the words stuck in his throt, which was right seein as they were not good words. But I see that Hiram had reached that stage of his impedelment, where he had to raise a leg, an I knew there was goin ter be offul trouble.

I allus think quick, I ran to the door an threw it open, go — go — says I to Rorer and the Health Gent who looked orful dazed; go — go — says I while there is yit time,— he's armored says I an not responsibel, well they got out quick into the yard; I cast one look at Hiram Cuckoo, still rastlin hard with hisself. I rushed to the parlor door an opened it. O sech a sad sight William, my foldin bed was let down, they had shooed the poltry under it an Par an them Hebrews was all spread out guardin them. Git them hens out an go, go quick says I, or you'll lose them.

The cross-eyed feller threw up his hands, but he closed in on Dick, an the other Hebrew lay on his stummick an pulls out two hens from under the bed.

Par grabbed up two more an I picked up the last, an run her rite into Hirams arms, who was standin swettin at the door.

Take her Hiram says I or Rorer will git her, hes layin for her; I knew by sayin them words that Hiram Cuckoo would never let go that hen while he had life. Then I opened my front door an got them men out with the hens.

The Hebrew went out caushus like till all to onct he spies Rorer an the Health Gent comin out of the yard, then he made a dash down the street as if twas fer his life, holdin that rooster on his chist with both arms.

The other Hebrew, an Pa an Hiram, runnin like mad behind him.

I was so wrot up an excited that I ran to the gate, a-ringin my hands, an jest then a butcher man came along in his team; he stops an looks fust at me, an then after the men runnin with the hens, an all to onct, like a ragin idjit, he hollers out, perlice, perlice till he was red in the face. That started a lot of boys after Par an the Hebrews, shoutin Stop Theef.

Well William Julep I got terrible excited, I wanted to tell those bad boys that the men warnt theeves, so I started an ran as fast as I could down the street, an O William, in a minute, the hull town was out, chasin those poor incent men, as if they was huntin down wild beasts. I'll never forgit it to my dyin day, an I prayed that no one would ketch Hiram or try to take his hen away.

At last, O joy, at the corner of the street a car came along an stopped to let out a lady,— I see Hiram git on the car fust of all with his hen, an Par an the Hebrews pile rite in after him.

I stood there pantin on the corner, with a crowd around me like I was one of them Salvation gals, an all of a sudden, a big perliceman came rite up twirlin his stick,—

Whats the matter says he, but before

I could git breath to answer, one of those bad boys says, they pinched the loidys birds.

With that the big perliceman turned to run fer that car to arest those poor hunted Hebrews. But I had presents of mind to grab hold of his coat tails, dont go mister I hollers, there not hurtin that poltry a mite,— they bot an paid fer them an they cant help pinchin them a little. Says I let the poor men be mister,— they have been hounded like wild beasts. They paid for them, paid cash fer five hens an a rooster. Then what in time are you chasin them for, says the perliceman. Well I xplained a little seein as how he was a officer of the law, an then I went home.

Benjamin Rorer an the Health Gent was no wheres to be seen, which was a good thing for them,— for I was mad William.

If I do say it, the Backup temper is orful, an I have my share of it. I dont git plum crazy like Hiram Cuckoo, cause my speech stays limber, but I was certainly mad that day.

An I had provocashun goodness knows.

Par an Hiram got to Thanatopsis an hour later. They said the Hebrew Gents got home safe and sound with the hens; but I am all through keepin hens, while I am livin here.

YOUR LOVIN MINT.

P. I. L.

Aint it strange when you stop to think of Dick an those hens travellin on the cars twict to take up their abod in Chelsea.

CHAPTER XXI

DEER WILLIAM,—
There is lots goin on here but
fust of all I must git to the part
that is leadin slow but sure to the mistery
that I hev allus felt has been a hovrin
over Molly Burt.

To-day I was scrubin the porch, when
a big ottermorbeel drew up an stopped
at Thanatopsis, an a lady stepped out,
sech a stilish lady I never see in all my
life. Not that she was titivated in silk
or satin not at all, she had on the plainest
dress I ever see, but it fitted her like she
was born into it, an she held her head in
sech a way. My lands, an ter clap the
climax she had a pair of specks on a handle that she held up bfore her eyes, an she
stud outside the gate an studied the sign

165

over my front door as if she was readin
the price of admission to the circus.   I will
admit William that I forgot myself an
stared tell I see she has turned the specs
on me an was lookin at Mint Julep as if
she was a specimin.   Well I aint no
specimin.   I'm   a   freeborn   American
woman an I dident jest like the way she
turned those speck on me an I stud up
an walked to the gate.

" Good morning, missus," says I, reel
naborly.

Well, William her shoulders went up
an the handle specks went up an she
looked me all over again.

" You have the advantage," says she.

" Of course I hev," says I, " you need-
ent feel bad bout it.   My manners comes
from the inside.   they are never put on
or taken off to suit the occasun," says I,
" they are allus the same an I'm sorry
that yours aint the same brand.   Now,"
says I, "your sight pears like aint good
for you have been lookin me over as if you
was tryin to find somethin that warnt

visible to the nakid eye, wot is it?" says I.

Well William, she dropped them specks quick, they was attached to a chain on her neck an they dangled where she dropped em.

"Madam," says she, "Is there a Miss Burt here?"

"What, Molly Burt? To be sure there is an if you know that sweet girl you're welcome specks an all." An I opened the gate an she walked in like the Queen o Sheba, an I escorted her up-stairs an I knocked on Molly's door, but just then, William, there was a dull thud behind. Ham an Eg had started to follow me up stairs and had landed on their heads. I ran down to see if they was kilt or maimed an the Queen o Sheba went inside. Well, bime-by I had to go into the entry again to keep Mamie an Tommy from payin a visit to Molly. You see she takes them in her room sometimes an gives them pretty boxes an things an they never knew she had compny, an was way up at the head of the stairs, and while I was calling

them down in a loud whisper I heard
Molly say plain as day, " home, I never
had a home. You were abroad all the
years that I needed one most. My home
was fashionable boarding schools, where
I existed from one weary year to another,
eating my very heart out for loneliness.
Why this little cottage has been my first
glimpse of what home might be." William
I did not wait to hear any more. I got
the children down stairs and I went into
the kitchen to do my work. But that
woman was up there a powerful long time
William an bimeby I went into the entry
to git Ham an I heard Molly sobbin as
if her heart was breakin. It stirred me
all up, William, for I hev grown to
love that girl as if she was my own. She's
so simple an lovin in her ways, so willin
an helpful an sweet that the sound of her
weepin set my heart thumpin queer like.
I was filled with animosity for that female, be she ever so like Queen Sheba, an
it came to me that I hadent ever axed her,
her name or business, sposin she was a

enemy of that gal. There had been a
somethin hangin over Molly Burt ever
sense she came to me an as she did not ap-
pear to have any natral gardeens, wasent
it my business I argyed to myself to watch
out for her intrusts, an not be havin females come around that made her weep
an sobb an when I came to this conclushun
I went boldly up them stairs an knocked
but bless yer they was so terrible excited
inside they never heard and I hear Molly
say " I shall never marry him."

" What," cried the other, " would you
refuse to do this for me after all I have
done for you. I have taken your mother's place, remember that, Molly, and I
am doing it all for your own welfare."

" My mother would never try to force
me to marry a man I loathed," said Molly.
Then the Queen o Sheba began to weep
an plead. " You must, Molly, you owe
it to me, to your self, to everything to
marry this man," says she. Would you
see me a beggar, Molly, cast into the
street without a penny."

"No, no, no," says Molly, "I have plenty, take all I have, it is yours."

Well, William, with that, the Queen o Sheba began to cry somethin terrible. "Oh," she says, "forgive me, Molly, yours is gone too. I did not mean to do it. I was led on an tempted. I thought it was for your good. I invested it with the rest. Say you forgive me, Molly."

Well I knocked again but they never heard, an then Molly gets calm. "There is nothing to forgive," says she, "I dont care a snap for the money. If it were not that it would be helpful to you now I would be glad, glad, that it is gone."

"How can I face the world in want," sobbed that woman, "Oh, the pity of it, the horror."

Well, William, she was cryin, an my heart was beatin, but I see that she was no enemy an it was none of my business, so I swallowed a lump in my throat an went down stairs to do my work. An at last, oh, sech a long, long time I hear talkin on the stairs an out I went again into

Molly Burt

the entry an the Queen o Sheba was jest
goin an my lands her face was all smiles,
she was feelin so good natured thet she
forgot to hold up the specks with the handle when she sees me, and at the door she
says to Molly, standin there orful pale,
"Good-bye, dear, be sure and come
early."

Then she gits into the ottermorbeel an
the shover shoved off, and she looks back
as smilin an self-satisfyin as if she had
not a care in the world, an Molly slid out
an stood on that little porch behind the
honey suckle vine, an gazed, an gazed, an
gazed at jest nothin an all to onct she covered her face with her hands an cried as
if her heart would break.   Well I let her
cry a spell but at last I couldent stand it
no longer, William, and I went out an put
my arm around her, "Molly," says I,
"what's troublin you, You aint never
told me your business," says I, "an no
more have I ast it," says I, "but we're all
humans," says I, "an the Good Book says
we should bear one another's burdens.

Dont tell me if you dont want to, Molly,"
says I, " but sometimes it makes us feel
better to tell some one about our troubles
an things goin wrong.   I hate to see you
feelin bad, Molly, cant you tell me like I
was your mother."

" Oh, I cant to-day, Mrs. Julep," says
Molly, gittin calmer, " but I will tell you
all another time.   I am afraid you will
think me a very silly girl," she tried to
smile at me an hide the tears, but they just
welled up in her blue eyes and rolled
down her cheeks in big drops.

" I would jest like to ask one question,
Molly," says I, " an that is are you goin
to leave here."

" Not to-day Mis. Julep," says she, " I
would like to stay for a few days longer
if you dont mind."

" The longer you stay the better I'll
like it," says I, " and with that she arose
and went in quiet like and up-stairs.

Oh what a pitty to see a pretty creature like this at a time of life when the
whole world orter be a smile grieven an

pinein. There is something wrong somewheres, William, of that I'm sure, but it
aint Molly Burt wotever it is, wotever the
mistery, she is sufferin for others of that
I'm sure.   Your own,

MINT.

CHAPTER XXII

THE MYSTERY DEEPENS

DEER WILLIAM,—
The very morning that the Queen o Sheba had called on Molly Burt and Molly had felt so bad that same afternoon the ottermorbeel drew up again an it had not been watin long when Molly came down stairs. O, she looked jest like a picture. She was all in white, but her face was whiter than the dress she had on. I went into the entry. "Wait a minute, Molly," says I, "I'll git a bunch of pansies," says I, "they'll give a little dash of color to your dress," says I.

Well she came into my settin room an I got her a reel pretty boquet, an I tried to cheer her up while I was pinnin it on, "you're dress is awful pretty," says I,

174

" an becomin. You look lovely in white, Molly," says I.

" I wish it was black," says Molly.

Well I tried to laff at that William jest to spunk her up a bit, " black," says I, " why any one would think to hear you say that you was a goin to a funeral."

" I am," says she, " to-night I bury all my hopes of future happiness." She looked terrible sad an I jest started wondrin wot she could mean an at last she says, " I'm going to a dinner party, that is all, dear, Mis Julep." After a minute, she added, " but to-night I am going to promise to marry a man I abhor."

" Then you are going to do a grievous wrong, Molly Burt," says I, " to him an to yourself."

" Not to him, not to him," says Molly, quick, " he knows it well, he is willing to take me at any price."

" Molly," says I, " dont you do it, you'll regret it long as you live, if you do."

" I must, dear friend," says she. " There's been an awful conflict between

love and duty and duty has won, not that
I deserve any credit for it," she went on
softly. "I am not doing it willingly
at all. Oh no, not the least bit willingly
though sometimes it seems as if I just
don't care and so Mrs. Julep I am going
to sell myself to-night for a little piece of
paper."

"Molly Burt," says I, "wot ever do
you mean?"

"Only this," she went on bitterly, "the
woman to whom I owe a debt has lost the
only thing she cares for in this world,
wealth, she was a rich woman, Mrs. Julep,
and she invested all her money in this very
Beruba Plantation Co. that has caused so
much sorrow. She not only invested her
own money, she took most of mine, hoping to pay it back, ten-fold. Well, she
holds a check for the entire sum of money
invested and when I give my word to-
night to marry this man, he will sign that
check and pay her every penny. It is a
bargain, dont you see," she said, with a

bitter little laugh, and then suddenly she covered her face and wept bitterly.

"Molly," said I, "dont cry, it cuts me like a knife to see you feelin like this," says I, "its all wrong, its wicked an onnatral. I'd like to see the woman git her money back," says I, "out of that terrible Beruba Company, but not at any sech price, *you* have no right to sacrifice yourself, Molly," says I.

Then she sighed. William how that poor girl sighed, but she stud up, William, and she drew on her wraps an she was gone, as there was a queer sinkin of my heart as I watched her an I put the children to bed, an I wated an wated an wated, settin there at the window behind that honeysuckle vine, an quite late it was when the otter drew up to Thanatopsis an a tall man in evening dress steps out an he helps Molly out. It was half-moon light but I did not get a look at his face because of the vine, but Molly seemed to hurry away from him. He was right at her heels and at the porch she stopped an said: "Good night, Mr. Somethin" I couldent catch his name, sounded like Frend. "Good night, Molly," says he, an then he caught her hand an bent over to kiss it, but Molly snatched it away quick an like a flash she was up the stairs. I wouldent be sure but it seemed as if I heard a low kind or sarcastic laugh from the man as he stood an looked after her. However he turned quick on his heel an got into the otter an went off.

Your lovin and sorrowin
ARAMINTA JULEP

CHAPTER XXIII

MYSTERY DEEPENS—*(Continued)*

DEER WILLIAM,—
The mistery is gittin deeper an deeper. The morning after Molly went in the ottermorbeel to that dinner party I went to see Mr. Storey in his office. Mis McPeak had been to see him an had spoke for me but I wanted to hear from his own lips jest wot he thot about the chances of me gittin back my money.

Well he was reel pleased to see me an I had a nice long talk with him about it an jest when I was goin I told him I trusted him cause Molly Burt did, an had come to him cause she had given him sech a good recommend. Well he looked orful pleased at that an seein as he was sech a good friend to Molly I knew hed be sorry to hear that her money was gone too

179

in that dreadful Beruba thing so I told
him.   Well William Julep his whole face
lit up you'd most think he had heard good
news stead of bad.   Are you quite sure of
this Mis Julep, says he.   Positive, says
I.   I had it from Molly's own lips yesterday, says I.

Well William that very afternoon I
was in my settin room alone as the children was gone to the water with mar an
par an Hiram.   Pretty soon Molly comes
along an opens the gate.   Well my blinds
were closed but I couldent help seein her.
I jest love to look at Molly Burt, she's
so pretty an her cloes seems to set on her
diffrent from most gals an tenny rate she
had only reached the porch, when the gate
clicks again and there was Mr. Storey.
Molly turned an looked so surprised I
thot she'd drop, but he came right up an
he says, " Molly," an she says " Jerry,"
an then he tuk her hand an held it an I
could see the color comin in the gals face.
Well says I to myself it looks like they
was sweethearts.   If them two aint in love

with each other I dont know the symbols, says I, an then it came to me that it was only the night before that she had gone to that party to give her word to marry another man. O, the pity of it, here was a reel, manly young man that I could see jest thot the world of her why hadent Mr. Jeremiah spoken fust, but perhaps he did, how did I know, an then like a flash I remembered how his face lit up that very morning when he heard her money was gone, an he says to me, are you quite sure, an he had lost no time in gittin to see her, and tenny rate, I was sore puzzled, an I couldent jest figger it all out an as they decided to sit down on the settee, I got right up an went into the kitchen or I would have been a eaves-dropper to have stayed as I could not help hearin every word they said to each other.

Well, while I was busy at my work about an hour later, I happened to go out into the yard an Mis McPeak came to the fense an told me that Scotty told her that Orrin Feather, the head of that

Beruba was going to be put to jail for fraud.

" You dont tell me," says I, an then I told her that the lawyer Mr. Jeremiah was on the front porch with Molly Burt.

Likely he came down to tell her, says I, for she has lost her money in Feather's schemes as well as you an me. Just with that I heard the gate click an I see Mr. Storey goin out. He walked away fast an never looked back. Well I was orful anxious to tell Molly about that man Feather so in I ran an out to the front porch to Molly. She was settin on the bench, and I'll never forgit the look on that gal's face. It was as if all that was sweet an good in life had suddenly gone from her for-ever.

At first she never noticed me but after a moment she turned and smiled at me.

" I think I'll go up stairs now and pack my things, Mrs. Julep. I am sorry to say that I leave here to-morrow."

" I'm sorry too," says I, an then thinkin to cheer her up a bit an git her intrusted,

I says, " did Mr. Storey tell you the latest about the Beruba Plantation Co?"

" No, he never mentioned it, what is the
latest, Mrs. Julep?"

" Why," says I, " that man Feather at
the head of it, is going to be put in jail for
fraud."

Well, William Julep I had hardly got
them words outer my mouth, when Mollie
Burt fainted dead away.

Mebbe twas the heat. I dont know,
but be that as it is, she has looked poorly
for some time so I jest gethered thet poor
child up an put her to bed an tended her
with my own hands. Well the next day
a high fever sot in an I hed to call in the
docter, an later when she cammed down I
ast her if there warnt some relative as
she'd like to see. I said as how they ought
to know she was so sick, an tenny rate
William at last she gave me the address
of her ant Mrs Lida Ryerson an tomer-
rer I'm goin to git mar an Bess Toby to
stay with Molly an I'll go an see her ant
if I'm livin.

But I do feel thet I'm on the track of that mistery whatever it is, at last.

In hast

MINT.

P. i. l.

I'm jest pinein to git you William so as I can talk this to you, cause theres lots you cant set down in pen an ink.

CHAPTER XXIV

MY DEERLY BELOVIN HUSBEND,
  Shall I ever forgit all that has expired sense I wrote you that last letter.

Well I started out the very next day to see Molly's ant, mis Ryerson. I found the street an number all right, the house has a brown stone front on a reel stylish street, but William Julep jest as I was goin to go up them steps the door opened an a man came outer mis Ryersons house. I jest gave him one look an I knew him an I would have known him if twas in the bottomless pit. William that man was the shoe string feller an I vum I forgot all about miss Burt an my errant

185

an I jest turned an follered him every step he tuk.

I had quite a walk you bet, an onct I allmost lost him at a crossin an came near puttin a fat man's eyes out with my umbrell thet I carried under my arm, but I kept his gray tweed back in sight an at last I was rewarded for he turns into a big buildin, an in I went after him, an follered him strait acrost the corridoor to a big room where there was lots of people, some settin down and some standin around the walls; he walked up an sot himself down, an I ast a little man at the door, says I scuse me sir what place is this,— this is a stock holders meetin says he, are you intrusted in the Beruba Plantation says he, if you are jest set down cause this is a mass meetin of all the folks intrusted, says he.

Well I did set down where I could keep my eye on that shoe string feller an then I looks round an lissens.

There was a man on a platform makin a speech again the Beruba Plantation, he

talked awful—he said it was a fraud from
the beginnin, thet they dident raise
enough coffee down on that plantation to
supply the help around the place, an a
lot more. At that a smooth face chap
got up an he began to stick up fer that
Plantation,— says he Ladies and Gentlemen, says he, the man what has jest spoke
is mistaken, says he, this could not be a
fraud, impossible, says he, with sech a
man as Orin D. Feather at the head of it.
Do you know Ladies and Gentlemen says
he, how Orrin D. Feather is regarded in
the West where he come from, why my
dear friends says he, they name their babies after him. Yes my friends says he,
that is how they think of him out in In-
diany, their dear little babies, says he. It
couldent go wrong with Orin D. Feather
at the helm, says he.

Well then another chap, tall with specs
on, jumped up an shook his fist at the
smooth face feller. You're in it too says
he an I can prove it, you travel around
the country says he, stoppin at the best

hotels, posin as a gentleman of leesure, with your money invested in the Great Beruba Plantation Company jest to boom the company in a quiet way, and you are paid a princely salary by the company to do this spoutin for them, an I know it, says he.

Well before he had finished the people got excited an they hollered out — Feather — Feather — he's here let him speak. Well at that the shoe string feller that I had follered stood up. You could have knocked me over with a puff of wind at the sight. He smiles kind of sarcastick like, an he said a whole lot in favor of that Beruba,— no one has denide says he, that we own these tropical acres, there are vast possibilities says he an let us reorganize — why says he, look at the men who have faith in it says he an own stock in it. He mentioned some names but a big light haired feller jumped up an said those men never bought a share of Beruba says he, but were made a present of hundreds of

shares for the use of there names says he
an I can prove it. Well Feather said a
lot more about these men an at last he says,
ladies and gents says he, I have nothing
more to say, by there fruits ye shall know
them.

Well William that speech an the sight
of that man riled me to bilin pint,— I
forgot every thing an I jumped up on
my chair an shook my umbrell at that
man. I dident come here to talk says I,
but I couldent let a chanct like this go by
an when that raskil takes to quotin scrip-
ter says I, its time I spoke up. an then an
there I told those people that the man
they called Feather was the shoe string
feller that hed come to Farnham years
ago an swindld me an all the folks outer
good money.

Well William fact is I made sech a
desprit speech, an I shook my umbrell so
it scairt the wimmen. I was gittin madder all the time an at last when I sees that
feller smilin at me, I hollers out you raskil, thet injuiced people to give up there

hard earnt money says I, an tells them to buy a piece of the earth at Beruba an git a income fer life, says I, I'll git my money back, says I, see if I dont, an I jumped over the seets to git at him,— after that pandemony rained, wimmen fainted, an men squeeled. A lot of them got me an held me back, an Feather cleared out.

An then all to onct I see a sight that froze my marrer. Direct oppsite near a post, was a man with a yaller tie an curly hair an a crowd around him. There was somethin familyar about his back an then an thar I see him shake his fist an raise a leg. There was no mistakin that sign, t'was Hiram Cuckoo on the rampige. I knew now wot business had brung him to Boston — Hiram was in the Great Beruba too.

O William Julep you never see sech a sight of pantin men an hystericky wimmen,— I'll never forgit it to my dyin day.

Then I cammed down an went home to my children. I dident menshun a word

to Molly Burt about meetin the shoe
string feller comin out of her Ants house.
But tomorrer I'm a goin to that house an
find out 'mong other things, what that
swindler was doin there. Mebbe he's
playin his tricks on the ant of this poor
gal.

Your lovin Mint

P. i. l.

Hiram never come back to Thanatopsis. I guess he was so mad he went strate
home to Farnham.

CHAPTER XXV

THE SMOKE-LADY

Wintop.

DEEREST WILLIAM
I hope your well as this leeves
me at present, though I've been
through so much lately I feel like a diffrent woman from what I used to be.
However I went to see the ant the very
next day after that orful time at the Beruba meetin an I'll never forgit that visit
if I should live to be Methusalem.

It was a terrible stilish house, sech pic-
tures an furnitoor an what-nots an things
I never see — I hed a mind to put my
shawl over a nakid statur left out careless
in plane sight of any mortal man thet
came inter thet entry.

Well I rung the bell an a young gal
came to the door, I guess she's helpin

192

there, an when I told her I wanted to see
miss Ryerson, she said as how I must hev
a card with my name on it — well thet
made me mad an I jest told her I was old
enough to go out without a tag, an a lot
more. I want to see miss Ryerson says
I, about her neece, Molly Burt an here I
stays till I see her, says I.

Well she said to wait a minnit, an she
went off an bime by a man with stuffed
legs an boys pants on, came out, looked
like he was a play acter, an he put up one
finger and beckened me to foller him up
stairs, he opened a door an med a low
bow and said, miss Julep, then he bows
agin an gits out an I walked inter that
room an there settin back at her ease, was
the Queen o' Sheba smokin a little seegar.
I'll never forgit the sight of her layin
back an blowin puffs of smoke till I die.

She waved me to a seet with thet seegar,
but I jest stud at the door an wouldent
budge. Take a seet, says she, no marm,
says I, I wont take no seet nor nothin else
till you quit, taint perlite to smoke in the

presents of ladies. O says she, laffin like, do you object to smokin. Not at all says I, do I object to smokin by them as was made to smoke, if a man wants to smoke thats his own business says I, he can git comfort an a bad liver for all of me says I, but when a clean female puts one of them little pizin things in her mouth, its diff'rent says I. Taint nateral nor American, says I. I hev heerd that them terrible Turkish wimmin smokes, well let them says I, the hethen in them has got to come out some way an I dunno what better way it could than in smoke, but I never surmised that *you* was a smoke-lady.

Madam says she state your business, your opinions dont intrest me says she in the leest. Mebbe not says I, if I was a smoke lady they would be flavered more or less with tobaccy, an be apt to leeve a bad taste in the mouth, they'd likely soot then. Look a here says I, Satan must feel right to home with smoke ladies when there smokin there not prayin. With that she straitend right up an says she I shall hev to ask you to state your business at onct, says she, or leeve my presents.

Then she threw away the little seegar, an I ups an tells her all about miss Burt bein sick at Thanatopsis an I told her about thet shoe string Beruba swindler they called mister Orrin Feather.

I warned her agin him, an I told her as how I hed seen him comin outer her house an how I hed follered him to the meetin an I told her not to buy shoe strings, nor let him injuice her to put any of her money in that Beruba on the promise of gittin a income fer life.

Well she seemed to know thet I ment it all fer her good, and she warnt a bad lookin woman, light complected with a big lot of hair, looked like there was about ten pounds, arraigned like a hay-lo around her head, the goldenist hair I ever see outside a wax lady on Washton Street.

Well then I went home William an I couldent help thinkin this is a queer world anyhow, there must be some good in thet Ryerson woman to be the ant of that

sweet Molly Burt, but think of her bein
a smoke lady. You should be thankful
you dident git her but did git your own

MINT JULEP.

P. I. L.

I allus felt thet I would hev made as
good a man as any male I ever met in my
karreer, but it never made me take to
smokin to try to prove it.

CHAPTER XXVI

MORE THAN-A-TOP-SIS

DEER WILLIAM,—
I was reel pleased to see by your letter that you was intrusted in Molly Burt an the smoke-lady an no wonder, for sech happenings dont come every day in ordnery folks lives.

Naow I am happy to tell you William that the mistery is out at last, everything is cleared up an I feel more satisfied than I have for months.

The very day that I went to see Mis Ryerson that evening I sat with Molly in her room. We talked until it was midnight, an she told me the story of her life. She jest took my hand an talked to me like I was her mother.

Its a sad story, an its jest as I expected.

Molly has been made to suffer for others. But to git to Molly's story.

It seems her own ma an pa died when she was very young an Mis Ryerson, who is her mother's half sister (they had the same father, but Mis Ryerson's ma was a play-actor that this man married when his first wife died) Well it seems Mis Ryerson, the half-sister brot Molly up. I fear she is a very worldly woman, an to make a short story she wanted Molly to marry Mr. Orrin Feather. A course that ant dident know he was a swindler, all she knew or cared was that he was orful rich, an he wanted to marry Molly but Molly would not have him because she did not care for him at all. Well it seems he jest haunted the house an he got her ant to invest all her money in the Beruba Plantation Co. The ant even sold her beautiful summer home to put the money into his schemes, he assurin her all the time that it would bring her back millions.

An Mr. Orrin Feather was offul kind to

the ant.   He has a elegant mansion at the
shore, called The Anchorage, an he puts
it at the disposal of Mis Ryerson, an her
neice for the summer.   I suspect that he
did this jest to have Molly under his eye
all summer because he is bound to marry
that girl.   Well the ant accepts an Molly
Burt went with her ant to The Anchorage, but she was dreadful unhappy there
all the time because her ant kept urgin her
to marry this man, an the more her ant
urges her the more Molly refuses till at
last one day Molly gits desperate and she
pleads with her ant that she wants to continue with her painting.   She is an art stu-
dent an she has a little studio in Boston,
so she leaves the gay life at the Anchorage an comes to the city to go on with
her studying.   An as she loves the water
she wanders down to Wintop to git lodg-
ings.   Well, she said, as how the name on
our cottage struck her fancy, she was in
that mood, she said, when life looked sad
an a lot more, an she liked the little porch
with the honey suckle over it, an last but

not least, I guess she kinder liked Mint
Julep. Well she was reel happy here an
everything went along nicely till that day
the Queen 'o Sheba (wich is her ant Lida
Ryerson) drew up in the ottermorbeel.
Her ant made her see that day that it was
her bounden duty to marry Feather, because if she did not the ant would be a beggar. If she did Feather agreed to pay
back evry cent, an a lot more beside.
Well, William, poor little Molly sacrificed
herself, as you know. That night her ant
arranged the dinner party Molly Burt
gave her word of honor to marry Orrin
Feather, an now comes the sad part about
Mr. Jeremiah Storey.

He an Molly had thought the world
of each other since they first met. He
was too proud to tell her because Molly
was a very rich girl an he a poor, struggling lawyer, who worked his way
through college, an has had an uphill fight
to make his way, but the minute he hears
that Molly's money is gone (an by the
way he doesent know she still has a for-

tune comin to her when she is 21 that the ant Lida couldent touch) but just as soon as Mr. Jeremiah hears that Molly's wealth is gone he is happy. He came to her an told her how he has always loved her an asked her to be his wife, an poor Molly jest worships him but she has given her word to that other. An when she tells Jeremiah Storey that she is going to marry Orin Feather, there was an orful scene. She never told him that she was doing it to save her ant. She says she let him go away thinking she was marrying Feather because he was rich an could give her back the fortune she had lost. That was the hardest thing of all to bear, says Molly, an she jest sobbed at the recollection of it.

" How he must despise me," cried this poor girl.

" Nothing of the sort," says I, " he loves you yet an everything will come out rite," says I.

" He could never care for me now, an it can never come out rite for me," said

Molly, terrible sad. " You dont know the man," says she.

Well William it seems that the ant has kept an eye on Molly all the time she was at Thantopsis, unbeknownst to the girl, for she told me so when she was here this afternoon, an she an Molly have made it up, an I guess that ant feels sort of gilty for the papers to-day are jest full of the Big Beruba Swindle an that man Feather.

There's a whole collum in the paper on his wealth, his fast horses, his ottermorbeels, an his town an country houses. O, I never hearn tell of sech a raskil, an jest to think that a few years ago he came to Farnham an swindled the folks there out of money in that shoe-string company. I tell you wot, it is a lesson for me long as I live an I'll never invest money in any schemes again.

When Molly's ant was jest outside my door she turned an looked at the name that I had painted an nailed over the porch, and she ast me how I came to name the cottage Thanatopsis. I told her that I

heard it at the perfessor's onct an I liked
it, and what do you think it means, says
she.   " Mis Ryerson is this a riddle," says
I, " it means jest wot it says," says I,
" some big words are kind of hard to say,
an the meanin is hard to git at," says I,
" but here's a name, Mis Ryerson, that is
as plain as your face," says I.

" Yes, yes," says she, kind of persistent
like, " but wot does the name convey to
your mind," says she.

" Sence it seems to be troublin you,"
says I, " its jest like this, a boy thinks a
lot of a top, dont he now," says I, " he
gits a lot of pleasure a spinnin of it an
showin it off, dont he," says I, " an wot
more natral than hed say to his sister or
some other gal, look at it goin Sis, aint it
fine an a lot more, now heres a nice cosy
cottage, an I can say to you, Mis Ryerson,
or to anyone, young or old, its wuth more
than-a-top-sis, that is how I figger it out,"
says I. " McPeak's cottage is named
Idle Nook," says I, " an that name is a
lie, cause she works like time from mornin

till night, an they aint a idle nook in the
hull house. Mis Kelly's cottage is The
May Flower, wich is not true either. My
name is the best," says I.

Well at that Mis Ryerson looked at me
reel serus like. Says she, "Mis Julep,
you are wrong about that name, it is not
at all appropriet for a cottage. The name
is a Greek word," says she, "an means a
View of Death."

"I dont care wot it means in Greek,"
says I. "This is America an we speak
the English langwidge an I know jest wot
it means in plain english an that's all I
care about."

Now William, did you ever in your life
hear tell of anything so perfectly redicalus
as to be puttin furrin meanins to plain
names like Sis an top. That Ryerson
woman is terrble hifalutin. I bet she calls
her underwear lingerins or some sech fool
name like a gal in a store one day when
I went into git some stockins for my
Mamie ups an told a reel nice gent I
wanted red hose.

" Nothin of the sort," says I, " Mister. I dont want a hose, an I aint never seen a red hose yit." Then she explained a whole lot to me but I declare I thot it was plumb foolish.

Your lovin wife
ARAMINTA JULEP.

Wintop.

DEER WILLIAM,—

To-morrow Bella Ball is goin to come over to Wintop an she an Henery are goin to take your par an mar up Bunker Hill Monument.

I think they are havin a reel nice time. The very fust mornin after they landed in Wintop I sent em out to take a bath, as your par said he loved the salt water an par has been in every day sense.

To-day in the afternoon they went to a corp house. A nice gent wot lives on the next stret was layin away his mother-in-law an I thot your mar would enjy the celemony, folks have, I never.

It is strange William wot names city

knowed that there was anybody dead in the neighborhood till I met Mis Kelly on my way to the store. She was all dressed up in her best an she stopped an spoke reel pleasant.

I'm on my way to the cop-house, says she.

My lands, says I, is anyone arrested.

"No," says she, "but there's lots that orter be."

Well, says I, if I may ast it wot are you going to the cop-house for?

Why, says she, to pay my respects to the family, says she.

Miss Goodcowski is wakin her mother to-day, says she.

Has she been asleep long, says I, dreadful puzzled.

"She's dead, woman dear," says Mis Kelly. Old lady Rosenberg is dead an gone an I'm goin up to the corp-house to see what the rabbit is goin to do."

Well, William Julep, I was that puzzled I jest could'nt speak an long last she told me that old lady Rosenberg was a friend of hers. A reel pleasant old lady, and she had been sick a week an then died, an when they is anyone dead in the house Mis Kelly says its proper to call it a corphouse, an when they are dead, she says, they're wakin wich I can't make out nohow. I did'n't want to press Mis Kelly too hard to xplain, but told par all about it. He says its furrin but he was reel curus about it an he an mar went in the afternoon. Par said it was reel nice an jest like any other buried service that he had ever seen. He said he got orful intrusted watchin a little man, cryin dreadful hard an most tearin his beard. When it was over par edged up to the man to condole with him. "Dont feel so bad," says par, "losses come to everyone, Mister."

"O, it was too much, too much," says he to Par.

"Well I know of course we all feel that way," says par, "but you'll git over it in time."

"Never," said the man, "I tell you I never get over dis." Then he takes par by the button-hole an he talks reel confidin like, says he,

"I tell you this, when Fannie Rosenberg marry Jake Goodcowski, I lend her mother $200 to swell de dowry. I'll never get it now, never, never, never."

"Well Par was dumb, he said his knees got weak an you could have knocked him over plumb. He says to me, Mint I'm gittin homesick for my own town for ding me says he, but this Wintop is a queer place.   Your own
                              MINT JULEP.

CHAPTER XXVII

A BUNCH OF PUFFS AND CURLS

Wintop.

DEER WILLIAM

Sech a pleasant supprise as we this day had. A trunk druv up to Thanatopsis addrest to your Par an we all got round an opened it.

There was a note inside from Bella Ball, an my lands, thet trunk was jest filled with bewtiful cloes for all.

There was a smokin jacket for your Par that jest ticklld him to pieces. Bella said Henery only wore it a few times, it was brown and Bella said the paper in her smokin room was pale blue, so she made Henery git a pale blue smoker.

Then there was a purple wrapper for your Mar an a pink one fer me. There was two fine suits of Henerys in thet

209

trunk, and your Mars eyes stuck out when she see them. She picked out a reel nice plaid one, orful large plaid, an she made your Par go rite up stairs an put em on. Well when Par come down we had to laff some, because you know Par is orful tall, an Henery some shorter, but Henerys soldiers are broad so the coat looked reel elegant, but the pants, Glory,— Par looked down at his legs, says he, I'm goin back ter short pants, mother, says he, I'm shrinkin, but your Mar see theres a good hem an she said as it would be a easy matter to let them down.

Then there was two of the handsomest hats in that trunk I ever see in my life, one for me an one for Mar. Says Mar it is bewtiful, but I have never wore any thing but bunnets on my head, says she, for thirty year. Well I jest grabbed up a little, round turban made all of vilets xcept on the tip top was a golden plume. The vilets were some faded but the plume was perfeckly bewtiful. I gave it to Mar an I took a grate big canopy hat loaded

down with birds an grapes.   Mar looked
kinder scairt of the turban, but Par says
to her, put it on, put it on mother, ding
me says Par if you wear that home, they'll
think we've been on a wedin tower, an its
mighty becomin mother, says Par.   Well
your mar looked reel pleased at that, would
you dast to wear it Mint says she,—
sertainly wear it says I, Bella Ball has a
perfeck taste for cloes, says I, an she
knows wot is becomin an she sent that vilet
turban to you because she knowed it was
the proper thing.

Well there was a stack of neckties in the
trunk, I never see any thing like it, all the
shades and colors any gent could wish.
Par said he had a good mind to start a
necktie shop when he went home; he said
as how he would'nt have ter lay in a stock
fer years in Little Acres.

Then there was a nice gray dress only
wore a few times, for Mar an other things,
a silk waist fer me an way down at the bottom of the trunk was a paper bag.   Par
went to open it an we all jumped,— thot

it was alive for a minit; it was only hair,
lovely hairy hay-los an puffs an bunches
of kurls, Bella is bound I'll have hair on
me.

But I know why she sent them, you see
I lost some of the puffs an cataracts she
gave me before,—'twas this way, one afternoon I had arraigned a bewtiful coffer
on me, I used the haylo an puffs an a great
bunch of kurls hangin down behind an I
drest up an went to visit at May Flower
cottage, me an mis Kelly was settin on her
piazza nice as could be. I was a talkin to
her an I guess in some way some of them
puffs got loose,— tenny rate they have a
terrible mischeevus little Tarrier dog
named Funze, Danel Kelly sets him ter
shake rags an things. Well Funze was
layin on his paws a watchin us, an all on a
sudden he jumps up on the back of my
chair an grabs that bunch of kurls Bella
gave me, an three or four puffs. He
shook those kurls tremenjus an when Mis
Kelly ran to git them away, he ran off
like mad down to the water. Mis Kelly

felt offul but I said let them go, an we haint never seen them sense. I told Bella about it one evenin when she an Henery came over.

Now I have more hairy puffs an cataracts an kurls etcetras than I can ever use, an I made your Mar take some; they aint a xact match for her hair of course, your Mars hair is brown sprinkled over white, an mine is kinder red, but I told her that dont make no diffrence these days, an when your Mar goes home I'm a goin ter arrainge a coffer on her to sute thet elegant turban wot she's goin ter wear.

Well there was a few other little odds an ends an in the note Bella said Par could keep the trunk cause it would be handy to pack his stuff in when he was goin home.

Bella is offul generous an warm hearted. I am reel glad Henery has done so well in the soap greese business. She's been a good friend ter me.

This is all from your

LOVIN MINT.

CHAPTER XXVIII

MINT'S FIRST AUTOMOBILE RIDE

DEER WILLIAM

I am goin to write you this letter before I say my prayers this blessed night because I want you should know of the narrer eskape you this day had.

You should be ticklled William for you come nearer to bein a widder man this day than you ever did before in your life, an nearer than I hope you ever git, while you got me.

I was settin on the porch mendin with par an mar, it was a reel hot day, an all to onct right before our eyes a reel stilish ottermorbeel druv up an stopped at Thanatopsis. I hadent ever seen the shover before, but settin in the back seet was Molly

214

Burt, a blue scarf round her pretty head an her lookin sweeter than ever.

She jumped out an shook hands an said she was glad ter see me an I said it was offul nice thet she hadent forgotten Mint Julep. Forgit you dear mis Julep, says Molly, no indeed says she, but I onct heard you say thet you had never been in a ortter, an so I hev jest run down this afternoon says she, an I'm goin to take you through a bit of our prettiest country says she, an I would like to hev mister an misses Julep come too says she.

Well William what a chanct thet was, but your mar looked kinder scairt an said thankee an she'd rather not, but your par rubed his hip pockit an smiled tremenjus. Well says I if mar Julep will keep an eye on Ham and Eg, I'll git my sun hat on an go. O says Molly I'm afeard your hat will blow to pieces, jest tie something soft round your hair says she, an come along. Well I ran up stairs, I dont own no vale so I tied a big red handcurcheef of yourn

William on my head and par fished up a little cap of Tommys thet jest covered his bald spot, an we got in, par settin in front with the shover an me beside Miss Molly.

Go kinder easy at fust says par to the shover till I git used to it, well that shover cast a look side-wise an all around an he began to work the pedal with his feet an turn the switch with his hands an right away he shoved off. Cashunk — we was down thet rode like a flash of light leavin a cloud of dust behind thet was like a fog settlin over Wintop.

Onward we rushed like Injuns in a wild race, houses an bill posts began to look dizzy. I see par git his chin down onter his chest an hunch up like he was a cripple, an every now an agin give a squeal right out. As fer me I was holdin onter the side of the ortter with both hands a jouncin up an down for all the world like one of them gals at the circus, an before I hed a chanct to ketch it pars hat was gone an we was miles ahead before par got his speech. Hi there says par, back up, back

up will yer, I lost my cap. Well thet
shover turned to par he talked reel snarlie
tween his teeth, looked like he hed a big
wad inside his cheek. Ar come off, says
he, does yer tink yer can find dat top-not
in dis maze. At this Molly who hed been
shakin all over with forbodin, though I
thot her eyes looked laffin like, says she,
stop a minit Mikeal please,— well Glory
he stopped so suddint thet I was bounced
up like a fizz cork.

The shover turned an looked at Molly
an she says to him, do you think we could
git the little cap Mikeal, if we went back.

Naw, says he reel forbiddin like, an he
pulls outer his pockit a leather cap an
passes it to par. Clap your paw onto that,
says he an your dome wont git a burn. He
talked orful peculeer. Thankee says par,
an he put on the leather then par smiles
kinder confidin like to the shover, hold her
in a leetle, son, says par, she's a fast one
aint she now kinder swift, says par. Why
she's a bubble she is, said the shover, now
yer see her, now yer dont, but we aint got

her goin yit says he, Ise only jest been
feelin her sec, an with that we started onct
more but William words fail your Mint
Julep for the first time in her life, an I'm
dumb when it comes to tellin about the
rest of that ortter ride.

I can only say thet no bird thet ever flew
the azure felt so light an giddy as me, till
all to once I reelized that the shover had
gone crazy, a suddint attack of Ortter
Vitus or something ekally bad had got him,
cramped his witals an made him hunch up
to look like a demon. He was tryin to git
to Hell William, an he most succeeded.

I yelled an hollered at him, but twas
no use an when I hed got winded from
screamin, I made the orful diskovery
that his eyes was shut, he was asleep,
William.

"O GAWD asleep at the switch,"
many a time I hed heard them words at
the perfessers an now I knew the orful
meanin. I see poor par writhin in agony
on his seet, as we went up one hill an

down another. For a second I shut my
eyes to pray, yes William twas as bad as
that,— then I hollered agin but twarnt
no use, I looked at Molly but she had
covered her face with the blue scarf, an
her shoulders were shakin tremenjus,—
thet poor gal was hysterrick.

Then I see we was nearin a steep hill
an the shover was gittin up speed to shoot
the shoots on the other side. I cast a
glance at par. A resined look was on his
brow, though the sweat was oozin out
under the leather. I got a wild longin
on me to keep the infernal from its mad
kareer cost what it may, an then an there,
I riz up an threw myself on the shover.
I klutched him round the neck with both
arms while I swung a leg side ways, to
hit his ribs — I wouldent let go though
he shuck hard,—'twas a desprit sight William, cause I allus ware white stockins,
though the stores are filled with black
ones. People inside should be white an
spotless. It has allus been a soss of pride

to me that Jamesey Allum was picked up dead at the town pump, but he was picked up clean inside an out.

Well I see the shover lookin down to see what was hittin him, he shuck hisself to git free of me but I held on like grin deth.

I heard folks shoutin at us an hollerin an then before I could reelize it that ortter was frothin in front of Thanatopsis — Par was standin on dirt rubbin his hip pockit, Miss Molly was laffin fit to die an I was tryin to git breath trembly like.

Thankee sir says par to the shover, I wouldent a missed it fer a prize cock, but I wouldent go agin fer a pair of them, says par reel smilin. Shake says the shover, puttin out his hand an squeezin pars orful hard, your a ded game sport says he, but your mudder, screw on de nuts, screw on de nuts, says he. What he means me an par dont know fer he's a queer chap an talks wuss than furrin.

I wanted Molly to come in an git a

cup of tea but she said her ant expected her back right away. And she said she never enjyed a ortter ride so much in all her life. It was fearfull William but grand. Twas like startin out fer Heaven, but feelin all the time thet you was jest missin the other place by a hair

No more at present from your

LOVIN MINT.

DEERIST HUSBEND

we got your letter tellin us thet you was comin home at last an tho you say you are goin off again to Canady soon we was all glad to git the news an mighty pleesed.

Your par an mar will now stay till they see you an then they must start fer Little Acres. I shall be sorry to see them go.

I have enjied evry day they hev been a visitin me. I like your par reel well — Him an me git on reel well together, your mar is a reel nice woman too though dredful proper.

She ast me yisterday if I warnt some older than you — course I am says I, I aint never denide it, an par spoke up an says to mar, an aint you glad thet she is — Smart of par warnt it.

Well William there ain't much news here. The childern are well though Ham got his front tooth knocked clean out the other day — Eg struck him in the jaw with a mallit, though twas all a accident.

The more I see of childern the more I wonder thet so many grown up folks hev all there members on them. Thet mine hasent been maimed fer life over an over agin is only due to the speshial dispensin of Providence.

Your pa thinks my Jimmy would make a better surgin or barber than anything an I guess par is right — Jimmy has a nateral gift fer cuttin, the only time thet boy looks wise is when he is whittlin a stick.

No more fer the pressent from your lovin an affecshunit wife

MINT JULEP

CHAPTER XXIX

MINT JULEP was a social being. She thoroughly enjoyed that friendly intercourse between neighbors which to her meant "runnin in" for a minute or two, at any time of the day.

She had as keen a relish for a bit of gossip over the back fence, as a lady of leisure might have at an after-noon tea. But more than all Mint liked to shine as hostess.

As she had once expressed it to Mrs. McPeak, "I do jest love to have parties an intertain, I could jest die intertainin'."

To invite the neighbors to come and spend an evening in her little sitting room, where among other things they could hear and see her talented family, was a wish

223

dear to the heart of Mrs. Julep. But alas! like most of our dearest wishes, it had never been fully gratified.

Now however, Mint believed that the time had come, when it was almost a duty to entertain.

William Julep was coming home and it rested with the wife of his bosom to make that home-coming an auspicious one.

She had fully made up her mind that she would give a party in honor of the occasion, and as she was finishing the white-washing of her little kitchen one bright morning, she planned out the whole affair with a nicety of detail that would have done credit to the late, lamented Ward McAllister.

As the woman of fashion has her visiting list, so Mrs. Julep had carefully gone over in her mind and made her list of those who were to be her guests on this memorable occasion.

She would invite Mr. and Mrs. McPeak and Mr. Voneye.

Mr. Voneye was Tommy's teacher, and

had always shown a friendly interest in her welfare.

Then there was Mrs. Kelly whom she had met frequently at the corner grocery, and her daughter Mazie who was always very nice to the children.

These with the members of her own family, including Pa and Ma Julep from Little Acres, would be about all that the little sitting room of Thanatopsis, would hold.

At last the white-washing was completed, the paint around the windows carefully washed and the windows " rubbed up " until they were clear and shining as crystal.

Mint regarded the result of her labor with satisfaction, and having carried the brush and pail to the back shed, she returned to the kitchen for the more important matter of the invitations.

From a drawer in the closet she took a box of pink paper, and from the top shelf, a bottle of red ink.

Thus equipped, Mint seated herself at

the kitchen table; taking the pen from its resting place in the box of paper, she proceeded to " try " it on the cover of the box; a few flourishes on this hard surface proved to her satisfaction that the pen was still " working " and Mint carefully started an invitation on the delicate pink paper.

Mis Kelly dear friend
I am goin to have a party to celabrate William Julep, my husbend, huntin wild beats in the Rockies an hes comin' home. I want you should come also your darter Mazie. You shall have a plessant evenin with
Mint Julep

Mint held this up and read it over several times before she finally put it in an envelope and sealed it.

It looks fine and I think it's a real good invite, thought Mint, but dear me what a lot of time it is goin' to take to write them all; and having arrived at this conclusion, Mint decided that she would write only one more, and that to Mr. Voneye, whose social position in the neighborhood, she thought, rather entitled him to the distinction of a written invitation.

The others she would tell by word of mouth, and " any way," said Mint, " it's a orful waste of time to write anything that you can say over the back fence."

But Mrs. Kelly's invitation was written and it was too good to keep, so hastily summoning Mamie, who was busy " hanging out " her dolls' wash, Mint placed the pink envelope in her hand.

Mamie was not unlike her resourceful parent. She was slight, indeed a very wisp of a child; a mass of dark red hair tumbled over a broad childish forehead; a pair of bright eyes looked confidently at the whole world; the small, retroussé nose, and wide mouth always grinning, hinted at a nature at once generous and mischievous. She looked eagerly at her mother and said: —

"What is it, Mor, another letter to Por?"

"No it 'tain't. I want you should take this letter over to Mis Kelly, you know the nice lady wot squints a little, lives next door to the grocery,— you know who I mean don't yer — was up here one day to see my hens —"

"You mean miss Schworer."

"No I don't mean miss Schworer at all. Miss Schworer has shingles an' is dreff'ul sick. I mean Mis Kelly, the stout lady right next to the grocery, wot squints a little, in May Flower Cottage, there now do you understand?"

"O yes now I know."

"Well then you go an' give her this letter, don't forgit now who it's for, Mrs. Kelly, the nice lady right next door to the grocery an' there ain't no answer; jest give it to her an' then run home here, I want yer."

Mamie started and was off like a flash, waving the pink envelope over her head, but Mint had only got fairly settled at the table to write Mr. Voneye's invitation, when the door opened and Mamie burst into the room, the pink envelope still clasped tightly in her small fist.

" Mor, she says she don't."

" Don't wot? Land o' goodness Mamie didn't I give you that letter to take to Mrs. Kelly? "

" So I did mor, an she says she don't and slammed the door."

" Mamie you tell me at onct, jest wot you did an' said," and Mint well aware that something was amiss, stood up and regarded her offspring with a very stern face.

" I ran all the way Mor, and I rang her bell and I says it's for Miss Kelly, the nice lady what squints, and she says she don't, and slammed the door."

" O Law, Mamie! You air enough to clip the wings o' Gabriell, an you haven't any tack 'bout you at all. I do hope you'll git it some way, 'fore you grow up, for I jest despise a female without it. A woman without tack is like a barrel with-

out hoops, all that's in her is bound to
come out an' she'll flop every time. Try
an' raise a little tack! Don't you know it
warn't nice to tell the lady she squints —
you must never tell folks they squint or
have a onnateral defeck.

" Jest the same if that woman's eyes
ain't allus tryin to locate her nose, I'm
tongue tied.

" Now give me that invite; I shall have
to put myself in her way an' make it all
right. I might have knowed that a fly-
a-way like you would have done some sech
fool thing.

" I wish I had sent Bud with it, nice, sensible, stiddy little thing that she is, an' I
will next time. Now git out."

Mamie did not need a second bidding
to get back to her play, but as she was
about to open the door, her mother said

" Wait, there's something on the pantry
shelf behind the sugar crock, I hid 'em
there from Ham an Eg — go git 'em,
give one to Bud an' one to yourself."

Mamie's grin was something very wide

and good to see as she emerged from the pantry a moment later, a doughnut in each hand, leaving Mint Julep, her arms outspread like wings of a great bird, writing Mr. Voneye's invitation to the party.

That evening after supper Mrs. Julep told the children about the party.

"Hurray," shouted Tommy, "will there be lots of good things to eat?"

"There'll be cake an' lemonade, Tommy, an' don't you take more 'n one piece of cake on your life, remember that, the cake is for the compny."

"Wish I was goin' to be the compny," said Tommy.

"You air goin' to help entertain them, Tommy, you stand right up when they all git here an play Home, sweet home, an' then set down an' say nothin' like a gentleman; that's what you are goin' to do.— You'll be all right I know, it's Jimmy I'm afeared of; I'll begin this minute to practise Jimmy, for I'm bound he won't be a dumb waiter the night of that party."

Jimmy whittling a long stick in the

corner, cast a doubtful look at his energetic parent.

"Yer aint a goin ter make me speak 'fore all those people, are yer?"

"Yes I am Jimmy, an' you can jest drop that stick an' stan' right up in the middle o' the room an' say the piece I've been larnin' yer fer weeks."

Jimmy laid the stick carefully on the floor, and arose with a most dejected air; thrusting both hands deep into his pockets, he advanced to the centre of the room.

"Well I never! I declare to goodness Jimmy, after all I have said, you would do it wouldn't yer! *Take them hands out o' yer pockets, quick;* now make the bow I learned yer, stand up straight like a man, throw out your chist a little an' try an' be some one even if it hurts yer."

When Jimmy found that he could not hide his hands in any safe place out of sight, he braced them squarely a little above the knees, then having tried in vain to recall the Mint Julep bow, he gave his head a sudden jerk forward, and stood

like a wooden image looking fearfully at
his mother.

" No Jimmy, that won't do, there's bows
an' bow-wows,— that looked like yer head
was on a hinge an' yer slammed yer face
at some one jest fer spite. You should
make it sorter graceful an' sweepin' like
this "—

Mint stepped forward in the act of in-
structing her young hopeful in the art of
making what to her mind was an ideal
bow; she had not however measured her
distances in the small kitchen correctly
and had backed into Ham and Eg, who
in all the innocent sweetness of childhood,
were smearing each others' faces with
black from the stove.

The twins were knocked down, and supposing this was some new and fearful
punishment for their misdemeanors, they
immediately set up a terrible howl which
had the effect for a few minutes at least,
of spoiling Mint's lesson in deportment.

At last quiet was restored and Jimmy
made another bow.

"Wot makes him throw out his stummick so," whispered Tommy.

"Hush Tommy, that was a real good bow,— that was wot the perfessor would call tryin' to emphasize hisself, which he has a perfeck right to do. — Now Jimmy, look the world an' the devil right squar in the eye an' say your piece."

If Mint Julep represented both subjects of this proposition, Jimmy could not have looked with more awe and fear in his boyish face, as he struggled through his lines.

CHAPTER XXX

" "MOTHER. who be that comin' up the beach, carpet bag, slouch hat?"

Mrs. Tom Julep of Little Acres, sitting beside her husband in the sands at Wintop looked up quickly and gave a perceptible start at sight of the young man approaching. "My sakes, father, it looks like our William."

"That's jest who 'tis, Phœbe, we'll not say one word, we'll jest give him a surprise when he gits near," but strange to say William Julep did not come near. Instead of taking the path that led home, he kept on his way and passed his parents without ever seeing them. Tom Julep jumped to his feet. "Come on Mother, we'll foller; tarnal strange thet a man ain't

235

going direc' home who has been away from his wife an' family all this time."

"They ain't his family," observed Phœbe, tartly.

"Wa'al if they ain't his then whose be they I should like to know. Don't ye lose sight of the fact, Mother, that when William Julep married Mint, he tuk her an' wot belongs to her; them childern are hers, they are bone of her bone an' flesh of her flesh, she has marriel William an' they are one, therefore ain't it common sense thet them children belong to him too?"

Phœbe pursed up her lips and did not answer. There was much about Mint Julep that did not wholly please the mother of Mint's husband. If she had the selecting of her son's wife she never would have chosen Araminta which only goes to show that she was not unlike all the other mothers of sons in this old world. But she had lived long enough with Tom Julep to know that he always had the best of an argument and in some mysterious way which she could never quite understand he gained his point and led her into the paths of his wisdom. Therefore she found herself hurrying along beside him, wondering and anxious because William Julep whose coming had been looked forward to, was not going home, and disappointed that this was so.

" Where in ternation is that idjit a goin' I should like to know," observed Tom, when William, after walking briskly for about a quarter of a mile, suddenly turned into a bit of woods. His parents following closely suddenly perceived a huge bowlder lying in his path. Behind this bowlder William Julep disappeared from sight.

Tom Julep stood as if rooted to the spot and ran a long finger through his sparse locks. " Wa'al I'll be dinged if thet ain't the strangest thing I ever see. Wot in time is he doin' behind thet rock mother? "

" I'm sure I don't know, father. William was allus kind of distant, he's orful bashful an'—"

Tom interrupted her with a chuckle. He rubbed his hip pocket and as Mint would have said "smiled tremenjus." "I have it, mother, come on, follow me." Tom Julep ran ahead like a boy and in another minute was on top of the rock looking down on William sitting on the grass wiping his face with a red handkerchief.

"Howdo, father," said William, looking up as if it was the most natural thing in the world for his parent to be smiling down at him from that lofty position.

"Naow, William," said Tom, stepping down from the rock, "I jest want to know what in tarnation air you doin' here? Here's mother jest arrived, she wants to know too."

"Howdo, mother," said William, still wiping his face vigorously with a red handkerchief.

"Wot are yer doin' behind this rock, William?"

"O, I'm just restin'."

"Restin', well I'll be dinged. You've

been restin' on steam kyars for 'bout a week now hain't yer?"

"Ya'as."

"Wa'al I should think you'd got so much settin' that ye'd want to git out an' swim on dry land somewhar. Naow it beats my sense of reason, William, that a man who has got the best wife in the world, an' who has been away for months, ain't a hurryin' home to her."

William looked quickly at his father a gleam of interest in his mild blue eyes, "Yer like Mint, father?"

"Like her. Course I like her. She's a woman in ten thousand. Why, ding me if Mint Julep was a man, she'd be runnin' a circus or the President of the United States."

During this eulogy Mrs. Tom Julep pursed up her lips but maintained a discreet silence. William's face broke into a smile.

"Ya'as I think she's right smart, father."

"Smart ain't the word. She's a born

genus, that's wot she is. Yer ot to be proud of a wife like that William."

"Wa'al I be."

"Then why in time ain't yer home a tellin' her so. Here she's been expectin' of yer, an' plannin' fer yer, an' stead of runnin' home to greet the best wife a man ever had yer sneak off an' hide behind a rock. I'll be dinged if it ain't enuff to make a woman like Mint git a deevorce."

"I didn't mean nothin', father," began William, looking scared. "I think a lot of Mint but I jest — wa'al —'twas like this. Yer see Mint is orful courageous. She could face a army an' give 'em talk. She likes a lot of folks round an' some-thin' to stir yer up an' all that, an' I al-lowed as how I'd jest lay low so to speak till it got a leetle dark an' then I would go home quiet like an' there wouldn't be no fuss nor nothin' an' no folks round to see."

Tom Julep thought of the party planned in William's honor and his shoul-ders shook with mirth but he said soberly,

"Git up, William, an' go home."

CHAPTER XXXI

THE PARTY

"WILLIAM I think it's no more 'n fair that you should say somethin' to-night when the folks git here. They all know I'm havin' this party jest for you an' it's only right an' proper that you should make a speech ter welcome 'em.

"They'll expect it; people have parties to bring folks out; makin' a depew is what the perfesser called it. Now a depew is nothin' without a little speech."

It was early evening in the Julep kitchen the night of the party.

Mint in a ferment of excitement, was putting away the supper dishes while "Par" Julep, and her silent partner, sitting on opposite sides of the stove, were having a quiet smoke.

"Don't you think Par that William ought ter make a little speech tonight?" said Mint.

"A course he'd ought ter."

"Speechifyin' ain't so hard," continued Mint encouragingly, "'tain't so much wot you say, it's how you say it; look at them politician fellers that all the people go to hear, 'tain't wot they say so much that counts."

"No," said Tom with a chuckle, "it's wot they don't say sometimes, thet counts. But jest the same Mint speechifyin' ain't so easy neither."

"It has allus seemed to me the easiest thing in this world ter do," declared Mint. "A man can say a word any wheres 'cept at his own funeral; any one with a live windpipe can make a speech. I shall never forgit one Saturday night, jest after William had come here from Little Acres; me an' him was doin' our marketin' an' we see a torch light wagon with a feller standin' in it makin' a speech, an' a great big crowd standin' around listenin' to him.

"Don't you remember that, William?"

At the mention of his name William looked up to see his spouse pointing a cup at him; he removed his pipe and bowed affirmatively.

"Of course you remember, William, an' the very words he said comes back ter me now, for we stood with the rest to listen.'

"'I tell you friends,' says he, 'something is wrong somewhars,' says he, 'something is rotten in Denmark'; an' they clapped an' cheered an' shouted an' gev him a pitcher to drink, they was so pleased."

"I bet he was a Democrat," observed Tom Julep.

"He was a plumber 'cause I heard a man say so,— but I shall never forgit them words, an' the way they clapped him for sayin' 'em —'Something is wrong somewheres, something is rotten in Denmark.'— I know 'em by heart. You know them words, don't yer William?"

"Ya'as."

"Well all you've got ter say tonight is stand right up an' tell the folks your real glad to be 't home, pleased ter see them. Think of that feller in the torch light wagon and say something smart like him; them words were easy enough, a child could say 'em, 'something is rotten somewheres,' ain't thet so Par?"

"Why thet's the whole campaign speeches in a nut shell," said Par, "ding me 'f thet feller warn't bright. But look a here, Mint, don't yer think seein' as William ain't much on talkin', thet you'd better let him go 'long kind o' easy like, an' never mind the speech? — You could say somethin' yerself, an' that 'd take the cuss off it."

"'Course I'll say something," said Mint, "but I know human nater an' I don't want ter disappint folks; they'll be twice as pleased if William says something."

"Now I have no more 'n time to put

Ham an' Eg to bed an' then help Bess
to dress the other childern."

The twins paddling their fingers in a
huge bowl of lemonade were immediately
pounced upon by Mint and carried off
upstairs, one under each arm.

"You'll git nothin' more than a lick
an' a promise to-night," said Mint, "for
I've got ter fix my hair an' lots o' things
yet 'fore them folks gits here."

At last the twins were snugly tucked
in, and Mint proceeded to make a hasty
toilet. She arranged her hair with the nu-
merous puffs, curls, and "hay-lows" that
Bella Ball had given her and putting on
her best black dress and white apron, she
descended to the sitting room to find the
children all dressed and looking fresh and
sweet as could be, thanks to Bess Tobey.

A wooden bench from the back yard
was brought into use and Mamie and
Tommy and Jimmy warned to sit on it
and "not git off," till told to do so. Bud
had a small chair all to herself; Mint pat-
ted her on the cheek and told the child

she was proud of her, because she was
" sech a little lady."

Ma Julep was given the rocking chair,
and to Mint's practical eye it was
very evident that there would not be
chairs enough for everybody. Bess Tobey declared that she and Mazie Kelly
could sit very nicely on the folding bed,
and if necessary they could borrow a few
chairs from Mrs. McPeak.

At this point Pa Julep appeared and
seeing the difficulty said not to bother
about him as he'd just as soon " roost "
on the window sill; but Mint insisted on
his having a chair and putting a hassock
under his feet, and Pa being tall, his knees
were very much in evidence.

Mint was still bustling about, putting
a finishing touch here and there, when the
first guest arrived in the person of Mr.
Voneye, the stout little German.

His broad face was rounded in smiles
under the soft Alpine hat which he waved
aside with a low bow as he entered the
room.

Almost on his steps came Mrs. Kelly and her pretty daughter. When Scotty McPeak and his wife arrived, a few moments later, a constant chatter was kept up,— Mint leading of course, with the little German a close second.

Suddenly Mint glided from the room; she rushed into the kitchen to find William Julep smoking peacefully, to all appearances utterly unconscious of all that was going on in the little sitting room in his honor.

"Why William Julep git up at onct, the folks hev arrived an' their waitin' fer you."

"Waitin' fer me?" asked William innocently.

"Yes waitin' fer you; good lands you ain't got on thet red necktie I bought, neither. I'll git it."

Like a flash Mint turned and flew upstairs, reappearing in a moment with the new necktie.

"Naow William stand up an' put this on,— you've got enough ile on yer hair

ter grease a steam enjine; but you look
real nice an' that tie is becomin' cause it
matches yer complexion.

" An you must say somethin' William,
folks allus do at a time like this; jest some
little thing."

" Wot? " asked William struggling to
arrange the tie.

" Why say you're glad ter see 'em, tell
'em how a man goes off an' is glad to git
back; think o' that politician feller in the
torch light wagon —"

" Look here Mint, why couldn't you go
in thar an' tell 'em all that fer me."

" William Julep! "

" Fact is Mint, I ain't feelin' real
spunky tonight, an' I'd kind o' like to go
to bed."

" Hounds o' Goshen! William Julep
if you was ter go to bed tonight, I'd be
disgraced fer life. Ain't I havin' this
party jest fer you? "

" Ya'as."

" There's no reason in this world that
would send a man to bed the night of

his depew, onless he was struck by lightnin' or chills an' fever or somethin' ekally bad. An' if you was struck William, after all the plannin' I hev done fer this, I'd hev you carried inter thet room with ice on yer head. Now come along."

The next moment Mint Julep appeared before the guests, leading in the conquered hero of the occasion.

"Ladies and Gentlemen," said Mint, holding William's arm at the threshold, "this is my husband, William Julep, who's been away as yer know, an' he's offul pleased ter see you all; he's goin' ter say a few words ter express his pleasure at meetin' yer, jest a little speech."

Silence and expectation now reigned supreme. Mint nudged William furiously and William straightened up and coughed, then coughed and straightened up again. Mint smiled into his face encouragingly and once more William coughed.

A sharp pull inside his coat roused William to action.

"Wa'al friends, I'm right glad ter be d' home agin, hope yer'll be the same. A man goes off an' gits back, an-an' goes off agin. There's somethin' wrong somewhere's somethin' is — is rottin' in — in — in Maine, an'— I allus vote the straight Republican ticket."

"Do you know what iss rotten in dot place, dot Maine? Brohibition," declared Voneye bringing his fist down on the arm of the chair, while William was led triumphantly to a seat by his proud partner, the guests still clapping his speech.

"You say dot you always votes the straid Republican ticket, my friendt," said Mr. Voneye, "if you do dot, you makes a meestake."

"Haows that," said Tom Julep scenting a political argument.

"Why are you Republican, tell me dot," said Voneye.

"Well," said Tom, "fust place my father was a Republican and my grandfather was a Republican, an' 'twouldn't surprise me if they was yit."

" So-o? a man iss Dutch, his fader was a Dutch und his great grandfader wass a Dutch — he couldn't helb it,— see? but dots not de way to git your polidicks. The Republican pardy iss good for someting, de Democratic party iss not bad for noding — und which I take? I don't know yet. I picks oud de best man ever time und votes for him — no pardy owns me."

" Wa'al we don't do it that way mister," replied Tom, " I'd vote the Republican ticket if they digged up the mouldin' remains of one, and put him up for President."

" Well I never," said Mint, who had listened intently during this argument; " Par is offul strong in his faith an' politics."

" You are wrong my friendt," said Voneye, " de best man de best way for me, and Von Groll find dat oud he came to dis country ven he vas only nine years old."

" You know my friendt Von Groll? " asked Voneye turning suddenly to William, who shook his head in denial. " Vell

he can pull your jaw oudt vile you vait,
mit shust his fist."

William looked mildly surprised at this
remarkable statement, but Scotty McPeak
who up to this time had maintained a dignified silence, laughed aloud.

"What's thot ye say?" asked Scotty.

"Von Groll can pull you oudt mit his
fist, he is a tood extractor, vat you call a
dentist," replied Voneye.

"I want ter know," cried Tom Julep,
"quite a feat!"

"No feet, he does it mit his thumb und
finger,— so."

The little German opened his mouth
very wide, placed his thumb and finger on
a side tooth, and proceeded to demonstrate
the movement.

Jimmy was so intently interested in this
performance, that he arose from the bench
and tried to look down Mr. Voneye's
throat. Mint coughed twice, and finally
had to pull Jimmy into position.

"Seems ter me kind o' dreadful," said
Mrs. Julep, who in spite of family cares,

did not lose her hold on the conversation.

" Don't it seem so ter you? "

Mrs. McPeak and Mrs. Kelly thus addressed, declared it must be " perfectly horrid."

" I heard tell of a man onct," said Tom Julep, " who could rub yer rheumatiz away with his hand. I allus thot thet there was some kind o' witchcraft in it; as fer me I've carried a hoss chestnut in my pocket fer upward of twenty year."

At this point in the conversation there was a dull thud over-head and Mint jumped to her feet and made a hasty exit.

" Guess them twins has fell outer bed," observed Tom.

" O I hope the little darlin's don't get hurtit," said Mrs. McPeak, while everybody looked anxious.

" No more than if they was inja rubber," said Mint reappearing just in time to hear the solicitous remarks. " Don't you never worry too much about babies; lots of things that would kill a man jest tickle a baby. When my Jimmy there

was a baby he swallowed a whole bottle o'
bluein'. I was washin' at the time,— well
I made him drink soapsuds, till his insides
had a regular Monday wash."

All eyes were now directed toward
Jimmy, who bore these glances bravely;
then all at once his mother said " Jimmy
has a real taste fer ellercootion; Jimmy
rise up an' say yer piece fer the compny."

Jimmy cast one look at his mother and
then evidently made up his mind that " if
t'were done when 'tis done, 'twere well it
were done quickly."

With hands thrust deeply into his pockets, Jimmy advanced to the centre of the
room, gave the title of his piece, and then
remembering the bow, stopped short,
gazed at his mother and jerked his head
forward twice.

" Charge o' the Li Brigade," repeated
Jimmy, after the second jerk, and then
being fairly started, he went along without a pause for breath or anything else,
until he reached " the mouth of Hell,"
and there he stuck.

In vain he went back into " the jaws of death," and repeated the lines over and over, all the while looking fearfully at his mother, whose mouth twitched nervously as she watched Jimmy's desperate encounter with his memory.

" That's very good, son, now go on," said Mint and again Jimmy, with a great gulp, repeated, " into the jaws of death, into the mouth o' Hell," but it was no use, that was as far as he could get.

" Well Jimmy let 'em be, yer can't very well get 'em back anyway," said Tom Julep coming to the rescue of the frightened boy.

This remark caused Scotty McPeak to laugh immoderately, while Jimmy backed to his seat, and in lieu of handkerchief which his mother had carefully placed in his outside pocket, he wiped the perspiration from his boyish brow, with the sleeve of his blouse.

The guests applauded Jimmy's efforts vigorously, and Mrs. Kelly declared that it was " perfectly splendid."

" Now Tommy," said Mint, " you stand up an' play Home, Sweet Home, for the ladies an' gents."

Tommy picked up his cornet and advanced directly in front of Mr. Voneye. Mint sat very straight, every nerve on the alert for the proud performance, which she felt in some measure would make amends for Jimmy's short-coming.

Tommy had on a pair of red trousers which Mint had made for the occasion out of an old shawl. An immense red bow stood out almost to his ears.

All the ladies present except Ma Julep, cast admiring glances at Tommy's trousers, and whispered, loud enough for his fond mother to hear, very complimentary remarks about them.

Whether it was the tight little trousers, and they were very tight, or the great bow under Tommy's chin, certain it is that Tommy looked ready to burst, before he even started to play.

The company were silent again, and Tommy raised the cornet to his lips, while

uneven strains of Home, Sweet Home issued forth as it were, in gasps.

As Tommy proceeded, his little fat face
began to rival the red trousers in color.

Tom Julep eyed the boy anxiously.
Everybody felt there was a crisis coming,
and it seemed to Tom there was a strong
possibility of Tommy's swelling to the
bursting point.

At last Tommy gave one long, final
blow as a sort of climax, when suddenly
Mr. Voneye, gazing calmly at the ceiling
all unconscious of impending danger, was
struck fairly on the stomach by a large
button from the little trousers.

"Gott you vas too dight, Tommy,"
flashed Voneye, risking a stroke of apo-
plexy in his efforts to catch the button that
had dropped to the floor and had rolled
away under the voluminous folds of Mrs.
Kelly's dress. That lady jumped to her
feet quickly and then everybody in the
room tried to get that button.

Mazie Kelly, her pretty rosy face
wreathed in smiles, cried " button, button,

whose got the button." All at once Jimmy who had followed its course with the trained eye of a marble player, suddenly pounced upon it and held it up in triumph.

If Mrs. Julep felt uneasy for a moment at this slight mishap to Tommy, the pride she had in his musical performance soon dominated every other feeling.

With beaming face Mint looked around from one to another, as if to challenge them to state whether or no they had ever heard anything quite so clever.

" It was perfectly grand, wasn't it Ma," said Mazie Kelly, but her mother was squinting so hard at the little trousers to see if they were going to hold, she did not hear the first part of the remark, and supposing that her daughter referred to the accident, said quickly, " 'twas orful, 'twas a shame, his troath was chokin' him, the poor boy, and med him swell up and bust his buttons."

" It's better to be too loose than too tight, hey Tommy?" said Tom Julep, " especially when yer not playin' a shrinkin' part."

Mint, smiling and happy, whispered something to Bess Tobey and they left the room, reappearing shortly with the lemonade and cake.

Tommy in spite of his mother's warning ate three pieces, and asked everybody in the room if they wanted theirs.

It was while the merry guests were partaking of the refreshments that Mr. Voneye, who up to this time had been the life of the party, grew strangely quiet.

Tom Julep said afterward that he thought the little German looked homesick. Whether it was the glass of lemonade, which he held on his knee but did not drink, or whether Tommy's playing Home, Sweet Home, had brought on this tender feeling, I cannot say.

He was the first to arise and declare he had to leave the " blessant compny."

" Gid more vind, Tommy," said Mr. Voneye, patting the boy on the head, " gid

more vind, and you be a'right, you will
yet be a great moosician." He then made
a nice little speech, at the end of which he
bowed individually and collectively to all
present. Indeed Mr. Voneye's speech and
generous bowing, set all the company bowing.

Mrs. Kelly began to drop courtesies to
everybody as if she were dancing the min-
uet; and after squinting hard at a plaster
cast of Miles Standish, which she mistook
for Voneye, she courtesied several times
to Miles.

Scotty McPeak shook hands with Tom
and William Julep and said he hoped they
were well.

Tom said he was feeling "tolerable an'
good as could be expected."

Then the ladies said they must go, and
that they had "enjoyed it most onusual."
Mrs. McPeak said she never had such a
perfectly lovely time.

When the door had closed on the last
guest, Mint, tired but triumphant, looked
at the man for whom all this honor and

glory had been consummated.   There was
a look of benign satisfaction on her honest
face and she felt that her husband must be
duly impressed with the grandeur of his
reception.

"William if I do say it, I hope you see
how your fam'ly done you tonight, an'
done you proud!   I'll bet your Mar and
Par was intertaint this night as they never
was in Little Acres."

"I'm bound your fam'ly 'll hev a cultur'
on 'em."

"I onct heard the perfesser say that lots
o' people in Boston was more intrested in
prize fights than cultur' but you'd never
think so if you see the money they spent
to git cultur' from the perfesser."

"William you have got a wife an fam'ly
that's got a cultur' on 'em an' that's all I've
got ter say."

"William Julep didn't you feel proud
this night?"

"Wa'al ya'as Mint, I did."

CHAPTER XXXII

"WELL this time tomorrer mornin' you'll be havin' your coffee
d'home in Little Acres," said
Mint, as she lingered at the breakfast table
with her guests, the morning after the
party.

"Yep, that's right, Mint," said Tom
Julep, "so we will an' though I shall be
glad to git home once more, I'm reel sorry
to be leavin' yer all as I have enjiyed my
stay tremenjus, ain't we, mother?"

"Yes, indeed we have, but I'm gettin'
kinder anxious now to git back. It's most
time I was startin' on my preserves. Wot
time did you say the train started, father?"

"Great Mespotamy! Did you know
the time was gittin' close," said par, taking
out his timepiece.

"Guess I'll haul that trunk out an' be-

262

gin ter pack. I've got lots more goin'
home than I had comin' here. I guess
mebbe you have got enough for the carpet
bag and trunk too, hain't yer, father?"

"Yep, I think likely I have. Yer see
we have all those cloes that Miss Ball sent
over."

"Yes, an' you orter wear that plaid suit
of Henery's home," declared Mint. "Mar
let down them pants an' I bet they're jest
right now, besides they will look reel nice
to travel in."

"Think so, Mint?"

"A course I do, they are reel stylish,
an' jest the thing for a gent."

"Well, ding me, I'll wear 'em if you
say so, Mint. I'll git the trunk and carpet
bag filled fust an' then I'll git the plaid
suit on."

"Mar," said Mrs. Julep, "I'm a going
to make a coffer on you right away. It is
too bad not to use up them puffs an' cataracts an' things. Jest let down yer hair
an' I'll fix yer up so that Little Acres'll set
up an' take notice an' reelize that you have

been to Boston. I should make it a pint, ma, if I was you to call around on every livin' soul in taown when yer git home for fear anyone would miss sech a sight. You tell em about Bella Ball bein' rich an' handsome, tell em that in these days in Boston, women are buyin' jest two things, cultur an' hair, tell 'em you've seen enuff cultur right in your own William's flock to last yer all yer life in Little Acres. A course I hain't braggin' 'bout Tommy, but you could say with truth that for his age the way he tutes on a brass trumpet is nuthin' short o' marvelous. Jimmy's mem'ry went back on him the night we had our party, to be sure, but nevertheless that boy has got it in him to be a Hello-quoshunist. There now, Mar, I dew think them puffs look lovely. Looks as if your hair was shadin' off to all sorts of colors and with that little turban it's jest grand."

"Well, Mint, I was jest thinkin' that if you'd jest as soon I'd rather have the big hat than the turbin cause it shades yer eye from the sun."

" Certain sure it does an' you shall have it if you want it. You look jest lovely, ma, in all them puffs. I bet the folks in Little Acres will jest admire to see yer, but yer don't want yer hat on yet. You're a goin' up stairs to change your cloes fust hain't yer? "

" Yes, I guess I'd better be gittin' ready too."

When Mint was alone in the kitchen she started in to get up a little lunch to be eaten on the train by the travelers. She had hardly finished her task when Tom Julep burst into the room, collar and necktie in hand.

" Look here, Mint, it jest popped inter my head that we had a trunk."

" Well, what difference does that make," returned Mint.

" Haow are we goin' to git it to the depot?"

" Why, par, I never thot of that. Warn't it stupid o' me. Yer see you didn't have it comin' so a course it never onct entered my head. Now you'd orter had a

express man call to git it. I wonder if
it's too late now?"

"Too late, nothin'. I wouldn't go without that trunk no how."

"Where's William?" asked Mint, as an
idea flashed into her head.

"He smokin' out back."

"William, William, come here a second," called his wife, running to the door.

Very shortly William pipe in hand appeared.

"William, I want you should run down
to Moon-light Avenue, jest around the
corner from the enjine house, there's a
furnitoor movin' man lives there an' mebbe
he could come rite up here an' take pa's
trunk. Run now, cause pa's in a hurry.
An warn't it too bad that we forgot all
about that trunk yesterday."

William departed while his father went
up-stairs to change his suit, but in a very
short time William returned and informed
Araminta that the man who owned the
furniture team could not be found.

"Naow, ain't that jest too bad," said

Mint, " how are we goin' to git that trunk
to the depot." As she said the words a
butcher boy stopped his team at Mrs. Mc-
Peak's door, and another idea flashed into
Mint's mind.

She ran out and asked him if he couldn't
take the trunk in his butcher team, but
the boy declared he had lots of orders to
deliver and could not.

" Well, ding me," said par coming into
the room, " but this here place ain't much
for accommodation. In Little Acres anyone would give yer a lift without askin'."

" I'd pay a half a dollar to git that trunk
to the depot. Seems too blamed mean
that we can't."

" We'll git it there if I have to buy a
wheel-barrow an' have William wheel it for
yer," said Mint, " but wait, I've jest had a
insperration. I'll git a team. P'r'aps I
could borrer one from Mrs. Kelley's son;
he has loads of horses an' carts in his business."

" What is his business? " asked par.

" His mar told me once that the city

made holes for Danel to fill." So saying
Mint threw her apron over her head and
flew out of the house and down the street
to Mayflower Cottage. She hurried
around to the back door and after knocking walked in to find Mrs. Kelly standing
at the sink washing the breakfast dishes.

"Good mornin' to you, Mrs. Julep, sit
right down," said Mrs. Kelly, her face
wreathed in smiles.

"I can't set down, Mis Kelly, I'm in a
dreadful hurry, an' I've come to ask you
to do me a great favor."

"Indeed I'll do anything I can for yer,"
said Mrs. Kelly, wiping her hands.

"It's jest like this, Mis Kelly, you
know William's folks are goin' to-day,
an' they have a trunk an' we never thot
of that trunk till the last minute, an'
par wants orfully to take it along on the
same train with him. He's got a big carpet bag too, an' tenny rate I thot seein' as
your son had a lot o' dump carts and hosses
you might let us have the use of one for

a couple of hours. I don't believe it will
even take that long."

" Well now, Mrs. Julep, if my Danny
was here, it's himself would take the trunk
for yer, but he's away at his work, tho'
I do think there's a cart out back. We'll
go out an' see. An' the hoss yer welcome
to along with the cart, only he's rale blind
an' he's kinder balky at times. Come on
an' see Maudie."

" Maudie " was the superannuated beast
that Mint was taken out to view in the big
barn, at the rear of the house.

" That'll be jest the thing, Mis Kelly.
Oh! I'm ever so much obliged, an' par
Julep will be delighted."

" Well, indeed, he's welcome to them an'
twenty more if I had them, an' a fine old
gentleman he is and the old lady too an' it's
sorry I am that they are goin' to lave us.
Can yer back up a hoss, Mis Julep?"

" Yes, indeed, I can. Wish I had a dollar for ev'ry hoss I've driv from Farnham
to Farnham Corner."

"Whist now, come Maudie, there's a good girl, come, now back up." So saying Mrs. Kelly backed Maudie out of her stall, and the two women, with no little difficulty, finally succeeded in getting the harness on, and hitching her to the dump-cart. Mrs. Kelly perspired freely over her part of the task and frequently wiped her face with her gingham apron. It was no easy matter harnessing "Maudie," and once the good lady lost her temper completely, and cried lustily, "back up yer ould divil yer, back up, or I'll break the ligs o' yer."

"She's some contrary, ain't she," said Mint, "but then hosses allus are when yer want 'em in a hurry."

Then Mint Julep took the reins and climbed up into the dump-cart seating herself on the swinging leather seat attached to two chains from the sides of the cart, and started.

"Yer look as natrul up there as Danny himself. Good luck to yer," shouted Mrs. Kelly, waving her hand.

"Good luck to yer" shouted Mrs. Kelley

"Git up now Maudie, git up," said Mint, giving the horse a slap with the reins. "Maudie" seemed to be in good spirits; she started ahead at a brisk jog that almost upset Mint off the leather seat, and caused a boy who had followed the cart to shout in derision. It was a very short ride, and the distance was soon covered. Mint rode up in triumph to Thanatopsis and stopped at the gate. She opened the door of her cottage to find the whole family in the sitting room around Tom Julep. "Mar" was on her knees trying to pull down the plaid trousers, but it was no use; par's red socks were plainly visible.

"Let 'em go, ding me, if I care," said par, "they ain't time to change my pants now, and besides ev'ry ding thing is locked up in the trunk."

"Mint, I hev allus said you was a genus. You've got a turn out fer us, ain't yer. Come on, now William, give us a lift with this trunk an' we'll git this trunk out."

Suiting the action to the word Tom Julep and his son carried the trunk between them and put it in the cart. When this was done Tom stood off rubbing his hip pocket, and looked at " Maudie."

" Well, I'll be dinged, that ain't jest exactly wot ye'd call a choice piece o' hoss-flesh, hay, William?"

" May be a better goer than a looker," said William.

" She's real blind, an' yer better not take chances," said Mint, " William can lead her when we git where it ain't easy goin'."

" Pshaw! yer don't hev ter do that," said Pa.

" Well, I'd feel lots better, if yer did," said Mint.

At this point all the children were begging for a ride, till at last Mint had another " insperration."

" Par you drive. William can lead ' Maudie.' Mar an' me can set on the trunk an' the childern pile all round."

" Well git in lively," said Tom, look-

ing at his watch. " There now are ye all
ready, mother? Git up, Maudie,
G'long."

It was a funny sight, and as the cart
jogged along loud was the laughter that
greeted them on all sides. Tom Julep,
his tall form dressed in the gaudy plaid
suit, stood up leaning forward a little
every now and then giving the horse a slap
with the reins.

" Mar " Julep's face was lost to view
under the immense hat she wore as she
sat on the trunk. There were many con-
jectures among the people who saw them
as to the whereabouts of the little party
in the tip-cart. Indeed John Gilpin's
famous ride of old never occasioned more
remark.

But " Maudie " began to lose the good
spirits which had sent her along so well at
first. Her steps began to lag perceptibly,
and all at once to Tom Julep's indigna-
tion she stood perfectly still on the road
and refused to budge an inch. In vain
did Tom and William apply all the arts

known to the trade to make Maudie " git
up." The party got out and the children
played tag while Tom gave vent to his
wrath, alternately looking at his watch and
trying to move Maudie. At last a carriage came along and its occupant, a
young man with a pair of keen dark eyes,
stopped and examined the stubborn beast.

" That horse wants a good feed of oats.
Guess she'll go all right then."

" She ain't my hoss, Mister," said Tom.
" I've got to git a train. Naow, what in
tarnation am I goin' to do?"

" Get in all of you," said the man.

Once again the little party piled into
the tip-cart, and lo, the stranger had looked
at Maudie's front hoof and the trick was
done before their very eyes. " Maudie "
jogged along and never stopped until
they reached their destination. What a
send-off that was. What shaking of
hands and good wishes and promises of
future visits.

" Good-bye, William," said Tom Julep.
" I s'pose you'll be startin' off yourself

pretty soon, when do you calkelate to go
to Canady?"

" To-morrer," said William.

" The idea," said Mint, " why didn't yer
mention it. I thot sure ye'd be d'home
another week or so anyway."

" Well why didn't you tell us, William,"
said his father, with a dry smile, " so as
Mint could git up another party for ye."

" I only got word from Mr. Ogden this
morning," returned William.

" Well, I should be orful pleased, son,
an' mother would to git a line from yer up
thar in Canady."

" An' I promise you *shall* git a line from
him," said Mint, " an' now best git on,
that's a whistle."

When the little party had shouted itself
hoarse, and every hand had waved the
train out of sight, Mint Julep and the
children got into the cart again and William drove them home.

CHAPTER XXXIII

MOLLY AND BESS RUN THE HOUSE

THE morning that William Julep said farewell to Araminta, on his trip to Canada, had been hot and sultry. There was not a hint of breeze in the torrid air and Wintop fairly sizzled in the heat.

Mint Julep was taking a batch of bread out of the oven when a breath of cool air from the window told her that there had been a change. An east wind as sudden and refreshing as an ocean wave on a sunburned rock swept over the little town.

She took out the browned loaves from the pans, and stood them on the kitchen table. Then she hurried to the door and looked at the children playing in the back yard.

She wondered if the sudden change

would affect Bud Tobey who had a slight cold. She called the child and asked her if she needed her little coat. Bud declared she was " nice and warm " and Mint stood there for a moment talking about the change in the weather.

From the open windows of the sitting room could be heard the sweet, childish treble of Bess Tobey singing " Rock of Ages " as she busied herself putting the room in order.

For a moment the picture of the girl's mother, as she lay peaceful and calm in death flashed into Mint's mind, and all that had transpired in that very room, where the child was now singing happily. " Poor, motherless Bess," said Mint. " Yet she is happy," and the thought came to her what a blessed thing it was that Bess *was* happy.

Her thoughts were suddenly interrupted by the postman, who had just come from McPeak's. He stepped to the fence and held up a letter for her. " Thank you," said Mint, " I wasn't jest

expectin' one, post-marked 'Farnham.'
Well, I never. Who ever has been writin'
me a letter from Farnham."

Clasping the missive tightly in her hand
Mint entered the kitchen, where she hastily
tore open the envelope and read the con-
tents.

" Well, I never," she exclaimed, again
and again.

" Sech a surprise. Bess, Bess, come here
a minute, till I tell you the news.

" Jest read that," said Mint, thrusting
the letter into the hand of Bess Tobey the
moment she appeared on the threshold.
" My brother Hiram is sick an' wants to
see me particular, jest read it."

" I'm real sorry he is sick," said Bess,
as she returned the letter which she had
glanced through hastily, " he writes that
he wants you to go at once," she added.

" Yes, right away," said Mint, " an' that
is exactly like Hiram Cuckoo; when he
wants anything he wants it quick; there
never was a man had so little patience.
Of course I know that it must be some-

thin' impartant but I don't jest see how I shall be able to git up an' git out of here, because who is to look after this houseful of childern while I am gone I should like ter know."

"Why, Mrs. Julep," exclaimed Bess, her pretty face eager and smiling, "I can look after them nicely, while you are gone to Farnham. I would like to do it."

"D'yer think yer could, Bess, all alone?"

"Of course I could, why, they are all able to do for themselves very nicely with the exception of the twins, and I'm sure I could look out for them."

"Yes, but Ham an Egg are sich imps of mischief, Bess, it sort of worries me."

"Now, Mrs. Julep, Ham and Egg are perfect little angels with me. I can do anything with those children, and don't you worry in the least. You must go and I'll do everything here. I'm so glad of a chance to do something for you."

"Bess, you are a good girl an' I'm awful glad you're here. I believe I will go.

" I'll git ready at onct too. Poor Hiram. He's had a peck o' trouble lately an' somehow or other he allus did expect me to help him out o' trouble, an' I should hate to disappint him now by not goin'. Yes, I believe I'll go. I don't spose I'll be gone more'n a day or two any way."

So saying Mint hurried out of the room to go up-stairs. She reached the little hall just in time to see Molly Burt opening the front gate.

" How do Molly. I'm awful glad ter see yer. You come right in an' set down. Bess'll talk to yer an' tell yer all about it. I'm goin' up-stairs to put on my black dress an' git ready to start for Farnham fast as I can go. Hiram's in trouble o' some sort an' has ast me to come."

" Oh," said Molly, with a smile, stepping into the entry way while Mint paused for breath. " Isn't that singular. Aunt Lida has gone visiting for a week and I got her consent to let me stay with you until she returns. I came all prepared as you see," she added laughingly, pointing to her dress-suit case.

"Well, naow, ain't thet too bad," said Mint, "there wouldn't be a soul to git you a mite o' vittles fit ter eat, an' yer never could stand the childern if I was away."

"Oh, aren't you going to let me stay," pleaded Molly, "I've never quite finished a little sketch that I made down here and I want to ever so much."

"Let yer stay. Bless yer heart. I'd like ter keep yer forever, but land o' goodness, Molly, you wouldn't want to stay in this place if I was away, would yer? Jest you an' Bess an' those noisy childern?"

"Wouldn't I, just try me, Mrs. Julep. Bess and I keeping house! Oh, how jolly," cried Molly, with the eagerness of a child. "It's what I've always wanted to do."

"Then go ahead an' do it," returned Mrs. Julep, with a decided nod. "I warned yer, remember that Molly, those children are perfec' imps fer gitten' inter mischief an' cuttin' up."

"They are dears, every one of them," declared the girl.

"May I have carte blanche to run the house," cried Molly, just as Mint reached the head of the stairs.

"There's no cart, Molly. Jimmy has a old truck, two wheels, ain't much good though."

"Thanks ever so much," said the girl with a ripple of laughter and the next minute bounded into the kitchen and proceeded to kiss the surprised and happy girl who was sweeping the floor.

"Oh, Bess, isn't it splendid, you and I keeping house. I've always wanted to keep house, real, truly house and now you and I can do it just like two sisters. No, not like sisters either. I've thought of something even better. I'll be the mother, because I'm ever and ever so much older than you. You are very young yet," added Molly with a patronizing little pat on the girl's cheek.

"I'm twelve," declared Bess, straight-

ening up and trying to look dignified,
" that's not so young."

" But I am twenty, think of that, Bess
Tobey. The audacity of a girl like you
talking to one old enough to be your
mother. I cannot allow it," declared
Molly with a pretty assumption of sever-
ity.

" The idea," said Bess, and thereupon
the very walls of the little kitchen rang
with the laughter of the two girls. Suddenly Mrs. Julep appeared on the threshold, bag and baggage, all ready for the
trip to Farnham. " Now, girls, I'm a
goin'. Take care of yerselves, and take
care of the childern. Don't let them git
cold. Bud is apt to ketch cold easy, she
needs extry wraps on the minute east wind
comes up. Make her eat an' watch Ham
an' Egg close when you go down ter the
water. Mrs. McPeak will be glad to tell
yer anything you want to know. I'll jest
run over there an' tell her I'm a goin', an'
don't tell the childern till I'm gone nothin'

bout it. I'll give them a s'prise. Naow
don't work too hard, girls, an' jest git all
the fun outer housekeepin' yer can git."
With several more reminders Mint departed to bid a hasty farewell to Mrs.
McPeak and to ask that worthy neighbor
to " keep an eye " on the girls till she returned.

Molly and Bess in the little kitchen proceeded to begin housekeeping in real
earnest.

" Can you cook, Molly?" asked Bess,
taking a spring that landed her on the
kitchen table, where she sat swinging her
feet.

" I can make fudge, lovely fudge," said
Molly.

" Oh, I don't mean candy. Can you
make biscuits an' things? "

" Biscuits. Oh, I never did but
wouldn't I just love to try to make some.
Lets have some for tea," cried Molly en-
thusiastically. " Hot biscuit for tea, and
I shall make them. Er, did you ever
make any Bess?"

"Oh, yes. I can make real good biscuit, and bread and cake and lots of things."

"Goody, then I'll get the pan and you tell me the ingredients to put in and let *me* make them, you can teach me how to make biscuit and things. That will be splendid."

"What, teaching the mother," said Bess, with a ripple of girlish laughter.

"Bess, we'll forget the 'mother' part of it when ever there is any cooking to be done, because you know, little girl," said Molly, gravely, "that I have never had any good opportunities to learn all about it. Here's the pan, now what shall I do first?"

"Well, mother," said Bess, with mock earnestness, "first take a quart of flour."

"A qu—A quart?" repeated Molly doubtfully.

"Yes, a quart, mother dear, why do you hesitate about a quart of flour."

"Why, it seems so funny to measure flour by the quart," said Molly innocently.

"One hears of a quart of milk or a quart of vinegar, but I always thought of a *barrel* of flour."

"Well, please don't for biscuit," said Bess. "It would be awful to handle so much dough and besides the biscuit would be heavy I know."

"Well then just one little teeny, weeny quart and here it is," said Molly, "and what comes next?"

"Now, sift it, mother."

"S — *sift it — sift flour*," exclaimed the girl.

"Well, why not?"

"Why. I know that people sift ashes but I never, never knew that they had to sift flour."

"Well they do, sift that twice," said Bess, laconically.

The biscuit making continued until Molly had actually rolled out the spongy dough on the board, shaped the biscuit with the cutter and placed them side by side in the pan.

"How perfectly lovely they look,"

cried Molly, "and isn't it easy when you know how," she added.

"The oven is good and hot," said Bess, trying it, "and that is proper because they must raise right up in the oven to be light and flaky."

When the biscuit were safely in the oven the two girls their arms around each other went out to watch the children at play.

"Be sure and look at your watch, Molly, very often, because they ought to be done in twelve minutes," observed Bess.

"I'm so glad you mentioned it, Bess, I'll look at the time every other second."

At this point Bud and Mamie, Jimmie, Tommy and the twins, surrounded the two girls and a jolly game of "tag" was soon in progress. Afterward they played the merry game of hide and go seek until Bess ran in breathlessly to look at the biscuit in the oven. The new cook, as it often happens with amateurs, had quite forgotten about them.

"Done to a turn," exclaimed Molly, while Bess held up the pan that all the

children might see what good things were
in store for them. "They would have
been done to a burn only for me," laughed
Bess, "while 'mother' played tag."

"Jimmy," said Molly, laughing joyously, "don't you think my biscuit are delicious?"

"They look good," replied the lad with
a grin, "if yer gimme one I'll tell yer
better."

"Let's save them for tea, and they
will taste all the better," said Molly.

When Molly Burt awoke the next
morning she ran to the window and looked
over the little stretch of Wintop that lay
before her eyes.

There was no sign of life in the cottages scattered here and there, but the
rumbling of a heavy milk wagon on the
street below told her that it was very
early.

In the distance a wooded hill loomed
a mass of blue and green and purple out
of the rising mists and beyond was the
sea, stretching away into illimitable shad-

owy depths. She smiled suddenly as the thought came to her that as a child she used to ask if the "big sea stayed in the same place all night." A sudden impulse seized the girl to go out doors and down to the gray sea before the little town was astir.

She dressed hurriedly and tip-toed out of the house without waking a soul in it. Molly's feet seemed winged as she flew over the road that led to the beach. Five minutes' brisk walking brought her to the water's edge and she stood and drank in deep draughts of the delicious air.

" It's clear and cool and morning sweet, it's good enough to eat," said Molly, thinking aloud, but the thought had no sooner flashed into her mind than it was followed by a more practical one, that of breakfast.

There was a houseful of hungry children at home. They could not eat the air, however tempting it might be to her in the early morning. Molly laughed softly to herself and immediately retraced her steps, reaching the little gate of Mint

Julep's cottage just as the front door opened and Bess looked out.

"Why, where have you been at this hour, I would like to know," said Bess by way of greeting.

"Down to the sea, Bess, and I found there all the sweet smelling breezes in the world waiting for me."

"Come in and make some sweet smelling coffee, please," said Bess, "I'm real hungry."

"So am I," laughed Molly. "Are the children still asleep?"

"Sound. Let's go around as still as mice, so as not to wake them. The longer they sleep the better. That is what Mrs. Julep says."

The two girls entered the little kitchen and were soon busily engaged in preparing breakfast. They had hardly completed the task when a warhoop from a room above told them that one little Indian was awake and on the warpath. In a short time all the children were up. What a busy time it was for the next hour

or two.   As Bess said afterwards they
had to be washed and brushed and combed
and dressed.   But it was all new and interesting to Molly.   She discovered that
Ham in some mysterious way had gum
on his hair.   Molly tried to remove the
sticky substance in vain whereupon Jimmy appeared with a scissors and informed
her that " mor always cuts it out."   " But
it will take some of his hair, too, if I cut
the gum away," said Molly, " and that
might spoil his head."

" Yer can't spoil Ham's head no wuss
n' it is," said Jimmie.   " Mor says so."

After breakfast the children were sent
out to play and Bess and Molly began in
earnest to enter into the joys of keeping
house.

For joyous it was indeed to the two
girls.   In a most systematic way they
aired the beds, cleared away the dishes,
swept and dusted, and then sat down to
plan the dinner.

Of course things did not always run
smoothly and there were many interrup-

tions.   Three or four lively children can
turn the best regulated household in the
universe up-side down in a few minutes.

Egg got a splinter in his finger and
howled so dismally after Molly had deftly
removed it with a needle that she let him
sit on the kitchen floor and make houses
out of cakes of soap.

Then Ham toddled in covered with
mud from forehead to feet. " I felled
in a puddle," he sobbed.

" I do think Jimmy ought to mind the
twins while we are so busy," said Bess,
" I'm going to tell him so."

" Say," said Jimmy, confidingly when
Bess at the door had reminded him of
this duty to perform, " when we're orful
good mor takes us to Barr's Float for a
picnic; we bring lunch an' have lots o'
fun."

" Wouldn't that be jolly," cried Molly,
coming to the door, " that's just what
we'll do, Jimmy, to-morrow, we'll have a
real nice little outing. Now you be a

good boy and don't let anything happen
to the twins while Bess and I are getting
dinner."

"Hurrah," cried Jimmy, turning a
cartwheel from the steps to the middle
of the back yard. "We're goin' on a picnic to-morrow.   Hurray, hurray."

In the early evening of that first day
of "keeping house" a drizzling rain kept
the children indoors.   When the supper
dishes had been cleared away and Ham
and Egg were safely in bed all the others
gathered together in the sitting room.
They played games and told riddles, with
Molly the life of the little party.

CHAPTER XXXIV

BARR'S FLOAT, a collection of rafts, boats, and old lumber was situated on a little curve of Wintop about a mile beyond the cottage. As it lay close to a pretty stretch of pine wood it was a favorite place for family outings.

Thither the little party from Thanatopsis Cottage wended its way on the morning that Molly had set apart for the picnic.

The twins Gresham and Egremont safely tucked into their carriage were wheeled over the road by Bess Tobey. The lunch for the party had been stowed away in the two wheeled truck which Jimmy pulled along proudly. One little corner of it had been reserved for Bud to ride on when she grew tired.

Room was also made in the twins' car-

riage for Tommy and Mamie when their
little feet began to lag perceptibly.

The day was warm and clear and the
little group of picnickers were bubbling
over with chatter and good cheer. Everything gave promise of a most enjoya-
ble trip. After a short walk devoid of
incident save that Egremont had fallen
fast asleep, the bit of wood was reached at
last.

A large rock served as a sort of hiding-
place for the wraps and the lunch, while
the party started to explore the wood.

When an hour had been spent in this
happy manner, they all gathered at the
rock for dinner.

Molly and Bess spread a tablecloth on
the grass and proceeded to arrange the
feast as daintily and artistically as possible. It was not, strictly speaking, a success, however as the twins thought it a
novel place to walk. They chased each
other across several times in spite of Molly's remonstrances and finally fell flat on
a little mound of jam tarts. Everybody

laughed because everybody was good-na-
tured and happy. The lunch proved to
be a veritable " feast of Lucullus " to the
hungry picnickers. When it was over
Bess and the children started to look for
berries leaving Molly free to sketch under
a great oak.

" When you get tired of that pencil,"
called Bess, " I hope you will follow in
our path and I'll show you where some
luscious blackberries grow."

" Thanks," said Molly, " when I get
tired sketching I'm going to sleep.

    ' This mossy bank my couch shall be,
    This knarled old oak my canopy,' "

added Molly, misquoting the pretty lines.

" Me is goin' shee Molly make picshas,"
declared Ham, looking back at the artist.

" Oh, no, Ham," said Bess, " we'll have
ever so much better fun, come with me.
We'll find lovely ripe blackberries."

" Me is goin' shee Molly make picshas,"
repeated Ham, stubbornly, and thrusting
a forlorn little thumb into his mouth Ham

stood still and refused to move forward another step.

"Let him stay," laughed Molly, when Bess all in vain had tried to lure Ham into the delights of blackberrying. "He'll be safe here," Molly went on, "I'll give him something to amuse him. Let Egg stay too if he wants to."

Egg did not choose to leave Bess then, so Ham wandered to the artist's side and was soon hanging over pencil and paper utterly oblivious of everything. Molly Burt sat with her back to the child, but in such a position that she could see his little brown legs. And every now and then in the midst of her sketching she made sure that those little brown legs were still there The minutes flew past and Molly sketched away. Indeed she became so interested in her work that she never saw the little berrying party returning until a sudden warhoop from Jimmy made her glance in that direction. At the same time she saw that the little brown legs were still in evidence.

"If you had stayed away just five minutes longer I would have finished my sketch," laughed Molly, as they surrounded her.

"Oh, isn't it pretty," exclaimed Bess, looking over the artist's shoulder, "and here is Egg behind you fast asleep. Where's Ham?"

Molly jumped to her feet. "Ham," she cried, looking down on the sleeping child in a puzzled way, "Why I thought Ham was there asleep. How did Egg get here?"

"Why he changed his mind about coming with us," said Bess, "and he ran back to you. I saw him myself reach Ham's side and sit beside him."

"But where is Ham?" cried Molly, looking around helplessly. "I never saw Egg till this moment. Where is Ham? How could he have gone from under my very eyes?"

A sudden fear clutched Molly's heartstrings. "Jimmy look around the woods and see if he's lost his way. Bess, you mind Egg and the others, while I run to the float."

Molly's pulses quickened and a nameless fear possessed her as she ran breathlessly toward the old float. In and out among the lumber and boats hastened the frightened girl but not a trace of the child could be seen. " Suppose he had climbed onto the float and fallen into the water," thought Molly. Oh, it was too horrible.

With wildly beating heart she ran up the steps and reached the very end of the float.

Shading her eyes with her hand Molly scanned the broad expanse of shadowy water but not a speck disturbed its placid surface. She looked back toward the land and swept anxious eyes over the old rafts, hoping for a glimpse of some human being that might have seen the child but the place was strangely deserted for that time of the day and not a soul was in sight. She could have cried out in her helplessness. Molly looked again over

the sea. A stiff wind had come up suddenly and stirred the placid water into
little choppy waves. She ran back to the
land. Perhaps Jimmy had found the
child in the woods. It was more than
probable that Ham had attempted to follow the berry-pickers. A sudden hope
filled her heart and she ran swiftly
over the float and in a short time gained
the edge of the wood. But Bess with
streaming eyes met her and told her that
Jimmy could not find a trace of Ham in
the wood and had gone over the road to
look for him. Molly turned like a flash
and retraced her steps over the rafts and
onto the float. The water! The water!
That must have been the magnet that had
drawn the little brown legs from her side.
Once again Molly's anxious eyes looked
over every inch of that pitiless deep. All
at once, far below the float, drifting between the mainland and a strip of barren
island she discerned a boat. At first
glance there was no sign of life in it, but
after awhile Molly thought she saw some-

Her whole soul was bent on reaching that drifting boat

thing white stir in the wind. The girl felt rather than saw that something was in that drifting boat. Unconsciously she clasped her hands together and prayed to heaven to guide her to it.

With a heart beating like a trip-hammer she ran back a little way, then jumped lightly from the float and waded to the nearest raft, untied the row-boat attached to it and put off as fast as willing hands could ply an oar. The tide was coming in and she made fair progress. A fisherman suddenly appeared on the raft and called to her but Molly never saw him. Her whole soul was bent on reaching that drifting boat and every stroke of her strong young arms brought her a stretch nearer. How she thanked Heaven that she could row so well and was perfectly at ease in that small row-boat. She had despised the fashionable boarding-schools to which Aunt Lida had condemned her all her school life, and yet it was to one of these very schools that she owed her proficiency in handling the oars. Stately

Southbridge Hall with its countless, shining windows and ivy-covered walls, its wide lawns and spacious dormitories, but best of all "Laughing Water" the blue lake nestling in its woods, that to Molly always seemed a thing apart from the gloomy school. What happy hours she had spent on its rippling surface and had learned there to row, to skate, to swim, and to handle a boat.

Molly glanced over her shoulder now and then to see how near was the quarry. The drifting boat had now taken a side course. Oh, if she could only look down into it. Suppose after all that the boat were empty. Suppose the child had climbed into a boat from one of the rafts and in some way it had drifted off. Perhaps he had fallen from that very boat into the cruel pitiless water. Perhaps even now his little body was floating out to sea. The thought blanched her face to an ashen hue and made her heart sick with fear. Her friend had trusted her with those children and she had betrayed that trust. How could she ever look in Mrs. Julep's honest, generous, mother's face and tell her that she had allowed her baby to wander to the water and drown.

Molly's lips trembled and the hot tears blinded her as she bent over the oars. She was so near now that she half rose in her seat and tried to look down into the boat, only to bend again to her work with redoubled energy.

One, two, three good stretches went the rowboat and then Molly looked up quickly to see something white stir in the drifting boat. For a moment the sight almost held her spellbound. Then she saw a little head, crowned with a mass of yellow hair. It was Ham. The lost child was in that boat alive. Apparently unhurt.

For one brief moment Molly's heart bounded with joy at the sight, then a new danger confronted her. He might even yet fall out of the drifting boat before she could reach him. And now he was rubbing his eyes; as if he had just wa-

kened from a sound sleep. Molly prayed
that his baby eyes might not see her —
yet. But alas, Ham was now wide awake.
He attempted to stand, only to fall flat
in the moving boat. He pulled himself
up by one of the seats and held on un-
steadily, while the boat rocked so badly
that every minute the girl expected to see
it turn over. A few more yards and she
could reach the side of the boat when the
child saw her. With a glad cry he raised
his little arms and leaned toward her,
while the boat seemed to stand on its side.
The heart of the girl in the rowboat almost ceased to beat. Then, like a flash,
something swift came between her and the
child. It was large and had white sails
and Molly realized in a dazed way that
there was a man on it reaching far out.
She felt an oar slip away from her hand.
Then all grew dark.

CHAPTER XXXV

WHEN Molly opened her eyes again she found herself sitting very comfortably in a little sloop that seemed to be cutting its way through the water at a tremendous rate of speed.

A man was standing opposite holding Ham in his arms. There was something familiar about the breadth of the man's shoulders and the way his head was set on them but Molly could not see his face. She gazed at the child now happy and contented while the man called his childish attention to the " big waves."

Ham was alive and well. Suddenly all the pent up misery and uncertainty of those terrible moments when she thought he had been swept into the water found vent in a burst of passionate weeping.

Molly covered her face with her hand-kerchief and cried pitifully. The man never turned. Apparently he was uncon-scious of her presence there and Molly felt very grateful to him that this was so. But the little sloop was even now trying to make a landing at the float. Molly ashamed of her display of emotion tried to dry the tears that almost blinded her. She saw a little knot of people on the shore. They were shouting and wav-ing handkerchiefs and then the man still holding the child in his arms turned to help her onto the raft. It was not until that moment that Molly knew that her de-liverer was Jeremiah Storey.

"Take my arm, Molly," he said in an undertone, as she stepped weak and trembling on the raft. The girl heard him and obeyed. The group of people who had witnessed the rescue pressed for-ward, but Mr. Storey ignoring all ques-tions found his way through the crowd to Bess and the children on the side of the road waiting patiently.

In an incredibly short time, thanks to
Mr. Storey, the little party still saddened
and subdued was on its way homeward.
Ham insisted on having his former position in the young man's arms, and carried his point triumphantly. Egg and
Tommy were put in the carriage. Bud
and Mamie rode in the two wheeled truck.
No one spoke. Mr. Storey tried in vain
to draw Jimmie and Bess into conversation with him.

The shadow of what might have happened still hovered over these two children who were quite old enough to com-
prehend its awful significance. At last
the little cottage was reached, and a look
of relief passed over the faces of all. It
was changed to one of surprise however
when the door opened and Mint Julep appeared on the threshold, extending both
arms in welcome. " Yes, I'm back. Saw
yer coming," said Mint. " How do Mr.
Storey, come right in. I'm reel pleased
to see yer, found the door locked, but
there's more 'n one way to git into a

house. Mis McPeak told me all about
the picnic. I'm reel glad you've had a
good time. What's the matter with "
Mint stopped suddenly and looked from
one to another.

"Mrs. Julep," said Molly, bravely,
though the tears were still very near her
eyes, "I did a dreadful thing to-day.
You will never trust me again with the
children, I know. Through my careless-
ness Ham might have been —"

"Look here," interrupted Mint, "one
an' all of yer, there's Ham an' Egg, an'
Jimmy an' Tommy, an' Mamie an' Bud
an' Bess, all present an' accounted for. I
sha'n't hear one word of what might have
happened. Don't want to hear it now nor
never. I sha'n't listen to it an' I shall be
dreadful put out if any one mentions it
again. I'm glad to git back, happy to see
you all an' that's an end of it. Git into
the house, ev'ry last one o' you childern,
I've got supper all ready. Won't you
step in a minute, Mr. Storey, and have

a cup of tea with us?" asked Mint, as the children bounded past her into the house.

"Thank you, Mrs. Julep, not to-night, there's a friend in his sloop at Barr's Float waiting supper for me."

"Well, I declare, they're at it already," said Mint, as a series of lusty yells issued from the rear of the house. "I bet those twins are tired to death, so I must run in. Good-bye, Mr. Storey, if yer can't jine us."

When the woman had gone Molly, filled with conflicting emotions held out her hand to the young man. "I can never, never tell you how much I thank you for all you have done to-day."

"Don't try," he answered, with a smile that seemed to light up his whole countenance.

The girl half turned to go but he caught her hand and held it in both of his.

"Molly," he said, in a voice that sent the warm color to her cheeks, "you are the bravest girl in the world. You would have caught the little fellow, I am sure; we happened along and reached him a little sooner, that was all."

" How did you know? " asked the girl.

" Davis saw the thing first, through the glasses. We were away over by the point and headed for you at once, wind and tide did the rest."

" I think the big sloop coming up so suddenly frightened me a little," faltered Molly.

" It was a terrible ordeal for you, dear. You need rest and I must not keep you. I am going now, Molly, but I want to see you very soon, may I come? "

" I shall be here till the end of the week," said the girl, strangely happy.

" Then let it be to-morrow," he pleaded.

" To-morrow, then," replied the girl, while the color in her cheeks came and went with every throb of her heart.

Raising her hand still imprisoned in both his own to his lips the man kissed it reverently.

" Good-bye, Molly, until to-morrow."

"Good-bye," said the girl bravely.

Suddenly a flash of humor appeared in her eyes.

"Parting is such sweet sorrow," she added archly.

"If you say that Molly, I cannot go at all."

"Oh, but you must. You forget the friend in the sloop waiting for you."

"I remember only that I love you, dear, that I have always loved you, but you are tired. I did not mean to say this now."

"It is better now, than to-morrow," flashed the girl radiantly, "because don't you see I am twenty-four hours happier already."

They laughed joyously.

"Then you care a little, Molly?"

"Oh, very much, for the biggest man on this little earth. He must be the biggest because I can't see any other, but I am going in now or Mrs. Julep will be out here to see what is keeping me."

She turned to enter the house, but the man still lingered.

"If your friend in the sloop knew that I was keeping his supper waiting," she went on softly, "he would probably scold all women in general and me in particular, but I would not care if he did — to-day.

"I feel that I could view the recording angel without fear or favor and smile at him, and now, I'm going."

She stepped lightly into the small hall but turned again and looked back at her lover.

He was at her side in a moment. "Do you really love me Jerry? Tell me all over again, but no, not to-day, your friend in the sloop may be hungry."

"I love you more than anything in the wide world, Molly," and folding her close in his arms he kissed her.

"I must go now," breathed the girl, and releasing herself from his embrace, she flew into Mint Julep's little sitting room, but when the click of the gate told her he was gone, she came back softly and watched his retreating figure until a bend in the road shut him from her sight.

CHAPTER XXXVI

THE TROUBLES OF HIRAM

WHEN Molly entered the kitchen she found the children just finishing their supper.

"Now," said Mint, a moment later, "you've had a good supper, an' I want ev'ry one of you to go out in the yard an' play. Molly it is time you had something to eat. Set down."

"Oh, thank you," said Molly, "I did not mean to keep you waiting for me. I'm real sorry."

Molly said that she was sorry but the radiancy of the girl's face belied her repentance.

"Set right down, Molly, an' Bess too, an' git a cup of tea; I have so much to tell you I don't know where to begin. I saw Hiram of course an' jest as I expected he

was in trouble, wuss nor that he was sick
abed an' in trouble. It's surprising," went
on Mint, when having poured the tea for
the two girls, she too seated herself, " it
is surprising how Hiram Cuckoo backs
right up into trouble ev'ry time he loses
his temper. He loses it ev'ry twenty-four
hours. Wust o' it is he finds it agin; I
wish he'd lose it some time fer good an'
all an' never find it, but as I was sayin'—

" Have another biscuit, Molly, thought
you'd like hot biscuit fer tea, an' I made
em soon as I got home."

" Thank you," said Molly, " I can make
hot biscuit too. Bess taught me."

" Well ain't that nice, but as I was
tellin' you 'bout Hiram," continued Mint
who was bubbling over with the news.

" Oh, yes," interposed Molly, " you said
he was sick and in trouble."

" The wust kind o' trouble, but I declare he deserves it. You see he was havin'
his barn shingled. Buck Wilson was doin'
the job, one-eyed Buck, got his eye put
out when we was boys and gals at school

coasting down on a double runner at
Peak Hill; well, he's a orful smart man
is Buck, he can see as good with his one
eye as most people can with two, an' ev'ry
body knows it, but that great, big med-
dlin', cantankrus brother o' mine, Hiram,
an' wot does Hiram Cuckoo do but git up
on the barn to look over the work."

" ' Here's a little place here,' said Hiram, ' that you left bare, Buck, must have
missed yer eye.' Now, ev'ry human bein'
in Farnham knows that Buck is mighty
sensitive about his eyes an' Buck says,
' you never mind about that, Hiram.'
' But hang it all,' says Hiram, ' it can't be
left like that.' ' Who's doin' this job, you
or me,' says Buck. ' Yer don't call that
doin' it, that's doin' me,' says Hiram, ' Yer
never see that spot till I called yer 'tention
to it jest now.' ' Git off my work,' says
Buck. ' What,' says Hiram, ' you order
me off my own property.' ' Git off my
work, or I'll throw yer off,' says Buck,
madder'n blazes. Well girls, I warn't
there but I know jest as well as if I was

wot happened. By the time Buck Wilson got them words outer his throt Hiram
Cuckoo was on the rampige. He raised
a leg when his impedalment got the best
of him an' he warn't in a good position.
He was on the edge o' that barn an' he
backed up, yes, girls, I am sorry to say
Hiram Cuckoo backed off his own barn
an' landed on the ground. 'Twarn't high
an' he didn't break no bones, but he's sore,
he's so sore that he stands up ter rest.

"Well now that ain't all either. The
wust boy in Farnham is Billy Wilson
(one-eyed Buck's oldest boy). He ain't
sech a bad boy neither ony he's terr'ble
mischievous, an' allus gittin' inter trubbel
an' doin' tricks on everybody. Well it
seems this is Billy's latest.

"The day before I went to Farnham
that young raskill went over to Hiram's
poltry place with his partner in villainy,
Johnny Reeves, an' he says to Hiram reel
innercent like,

"'Hiram,' says he, 'Johnny an' me has

jest stumbled right on to a discovery that will revolutionize the poltry business, an' make you a millionaire.'

" ' So? ' says Hiram, ' yer don't mean it.'

" ' Yep,' says Billy, ' it's wonderful, it's one o' them simple things that is right under yer nose all the time but no one has ever thot of applyin' it, jest like electricity an' sewing machines, an' all that,' says Billy, ' wich some folks has made a fortune on. Now,' says Billy, ' we know it but we are not in the poltry raisin' business, so it ain't much good to us, but it's wuth a fortune to them that is in the business. Now Hiram we are willin' to give the information to anyone that makes it wuth our while.'

" ' Don't take no stock in you, Billy,' says my brother Hiram, ' guess I don't want it.'

" ' All right,' says Billy, ' it don't make no difference to us; we came here fust cause it was nearest. Now we'll go over to Sam Blake's. Bet he'll jump at it.'

"Now, girls, there is a little rivalry in Farnham between Hiram an' Sam an' folks know it.

"'Well what's the natur of this thing?' says Hiram, gittin' intrusted.

"'It's ter hatch out chickens,' says Billy. 'Incubators cost a lot of money but our scheme, wot we jest stumbled into, don't cost a cent, can be picked up off the street an' used, so ter speak.'

"'How much do you want for the information?' says Hiram, fallin' right into the trap.

"'Well,' says Billy, 'seein' it's you, we'll let you make us an offer; we haven't been to any of the other fellers yet.'

"'But hang it all,' says Hiram, 'how can I make you an offer when I don't even know wot it is or anything about it.'

"'Well now, look a here,' says Billy, 'Johnny an' me ain't goin' to give away a secret like that for nothin'.' Says he, 'to-morrow Johnny an' me is goin' campin' up in the woods an' we want a good chicken to broil. Give us a chicken an'

we'll let you in on the secret. You can
pay the money later if yer want ter do it
thet way.'

"Well Hiram thot awhile an' long last
he goes an' kills one o' his best chickens
an' all the while he was cleanin' it Billy
was rhapsodeezin' over his discovery an'
there is no denyin' that Hiram was terri-
bly intrusted. Well at last he hands that
chicken, plucked an' cleaned, over to
Billy.

"'Now,' says he, 'wot is it, out with
it. I'm ready to hear,' says he, 'what
have you discovered to hatch out chickens.'

"'Yer won't breathe it?' says Billy,
putting that fresh-killed chicken under his
coat. 'You'll promise, Hiram, that you
won't tell a livin' soul?'

"'No,' says Hiram, 'you can trust me;
if it's a good thing, why, I'm willing to
do the squar thing by yer.'

"'Remember,' says Billy, 'it's one o'
them simple things that is right under yer
nose.'

" ' Yes, yes,' says Hiram.

" ' An' no one has ever thot of it but me, remember that,' says Billy.

" ' Well, go ahead, go ahead,' says Hiram, gettin' restless.

" ' Don't cost a cent! cheaper than incubators! picked up in the street!' went on Billy.

" ' Hang yer, w-w-wot is it?' cried Hiram.

" ' Cats,' says Billy, ' nice warm fur, set 'em on the eggs an' let 'em do the business.'

" Well, Billy got out 'fore Hiram could git at him, but Hiram is bilin' with rage an' I found him with a terrible cold on his chist an' he alone in the house an' stead o' nursing that cold he was nursin' his wrath. He told me he was goin' to sue Buck Wilson an' a lot more. Well, if I do say it me an' Peggy Barnes was the only two humans that knew how to cam Hiram Cuckoo Backup. I coaxed him inter bed. I got plasters an' I fixed him up an' when I had him where he couldn't

move without hurting hisself I talked
commonsense at him, an' I left him feelin'
reel comfortable. Naow, girls, I want to
do jest one thing, to-morrer, I want to
go over to Chelsea an' tell the hull story
to Bella Ball; me an her was girls together, you know, orful romansin girl
was Bella, married reel well, Henery
Ball, in the soap greese business.

"I thot as how ye'd jest like ter house
keep another day."

"Bess and I will do ev'rything," cried
Molly.

"Yes, I'm in luck. I'll go over, an'
see her fust thing. I'm jest dyin' ter tell
her the news o' Farnham. Mary Bassett
has twins and John Bassett was so pleased
he's writ a letter to President Rooseveldt
to tell him that one is goin' ter be called
Theodore and the other Theodora. Deacon Wells, posin' as a teetotaler fer forty
years, was found wond'rin' near Still
Creek with a jug o' hard cider. Abe Bur-
ton had a orful time to git him home.
Deacon said he was lookin' fer a barrl o'

paint. 'Wot fer,' says Abe, 'ter paint yer house?' 'Ter paint the town,' says the Deacon, cuttin' up an' yellin' for all the world like them college chaps. Oh it was orful, Farnham ain't got over it yit. But wust of all is the Carys. Oh, I'm jest dyin' ter tell Bella about them. Yer see, girls, them Carys are a terrible shiftless family livin' on the edge o' the town from the Granther (that's the old man) down to the very youngest a pair o' shock headed twins. There's eleven all told, an' Mary Cary is the oldest child, she's a big strong gal bout thirty.

"Well, it seems my Aunt Lize was short handed an' she wanted Mary to come over an' help an' Mary did. But one afternoon, Mary went home jest fer a little visit an' tho she promised Ant Liza she'd be back that very night, she never showed up fer three days when Ant Liza's steam power, an' it was something tremejus, hed most given out.

"'For goodness' sake,' says Ant Liza, 'where hev you been Mary? I hev been

waiting three days fer yer.' Says Mary,
' I couldn't come no sooner cause Grandther died, that is,' says she, ' we thot he was
dead.' ' Come in an' go to work Mary,'
says Ant Liza, ' I allus knew Grandther
Cary was slow but I never thot he'd take
three days to die in hayin' time.'

" Well, it seems Grandther wasn't dead
at all. They called in a young medicin'
doctor stayin' at the hotel an' he said it was
jest a commondose state; most oncommon
dose o' sleep it sems ter me ter last three
days, an' tenny rate Mary stayed on helpin' till the end o' the week, when she went
home agin an' never showed up at Ant
Liza's fer five days.

" It seems the Carys hed a party an' cel-
ebrated their golden weddin' this time, tho
folks said the only golden thing about the
hul party was Hiram Cary's buck tooth
that he had plugged sideways with gold
onct an' he allus wore a perpetshal grin
jest so folks would see it shine. Well,
it seems that after the golden weddin'
Grandther went out an' let a mule kick

him an' he really did die this time. Guess that weddin' finished him an' tenny rate, Mary came back to Ant Liza's the day after the funeral. Ant Liza met her at the door. Never a word said Mary Cary 'bout their golden weddin' an' all the celebratin'. She jest stood at the door an' says she ' I couldn't come no sooner,' says she, ' cause yer know Grandther died.'

" ' He did! ' says Ant Liza, who was orful outspoken. ' I thot he was slow,' says she, ' but after all I guess he was the most commodatin' corpse in the kaounty; come in Mary an' git to work.'

" Then there's Bess Holliday; she's jest came home from a female college. She don't b'lieve in marryin' or buryin' or nothin'. At fust the Hollidays felt jest orful 'bout it an' they went an' told Mr. Godwin. He's reel wise an' sensibel, says he; ' them symtoms ain't dangerous,' says he; ' Bess'l find herself all in good time,' says he; but Ant Liza says to me, ' Mint,' says she, in her outspoken way: ' a little learnin' is a dangrous thing,' says she."

CHAPTER XXXVII

MACHINE-OIL SALAD AND LOVE

"NOW, good-bye, girls, I shall be back real early," said Mrs. Julep the following day, as she started for Chelsea to tell the latest Farnham news to Bella Ball. "Look out for yerselves an' look out for the childern an' I think p'r'aps it would be jest as well to-day to keep 'em away from the water."

"The water," echoed Molly when the door was shut and Mint had gone. "I shall follow Ham and Egg to-day as if I were their visible guardian angel."

"Oh, that won't be necessary," laughed Bess, "they have a nice, long nap every afternoon, and they are safe out of harm's way then. Do you know what they like very much, and what keeps them interested," Bess went on, "a tent. If you

make up any old kind of a tent in that
back yard they play lovely together."

"We'll do it," said Molly. "I'll take a
quilt and pin it across the lines and have
the sides made of sheets."

The idea worked beautifully. The im-
provised tent was a "wigwam" the children "live injuns" and all sorts of delights were planned and executed, but
Molly Burt never let five minutes pass
the entire morning without making sure
that the twins were at play with the others.
It was not until Bess got them ready for
their nap after dinner that Molly's vigil
relaxed. Then she tripped up-stairs to
her room and looked over her wardrobe.
Some one very dear was coming and
Molly wanted to don her prettiest gown.
She had brought just as few clothes as
possible for the short week, but among
them was her sweet-brier muslin.

"I'm so glad I have it with me,"
thought the girl, who loved pretty dainty
things.

Molly was very happy and she lingered

over her toilet as if she found it no un-
pleasant task. The soft, brown masses
of her hair that had been severely braided
during the busy house-keeping hours
were twisted into a fanciful coil on the top
of her head. The pretty muslin was put
on with its ribbons and ruffles and laces.
Molly smiled at the radiant girl reflected
in the little mirror and went down stairs,
just as a click of the gate told her " he "
was coming, but Mr. Storey was not
alone. Mrs. Davis and little Freddie
Tobey, the picture of health and childish
grace, were with him.

"We want you to come for a sail,
Molly," said the man when greetings had
been exchanged. " Mr. Davis is waiting
for us."

"There's a stiff wind," observed the
woman, " it will be fine, I think, this afternoon, and Freddie is going to have his
first sail," she added, beaming down on
the child.

"Oh, I'm so sorry, I cannot go with
you," said Molly. "Mrs. Julep has gone

to Chelsea this afternoon, and I couldn't
leave the children, you know."

Mr. Storey's face fell. The glory of
the sail was gone if Molly could not share
it with him. "Couldn't Bess manage all
right till you get back," he ventured.

"Oh, I wouldn't want her to. It would
be too much to leave them all to her," said
Molly, "she is only a child herself. But
never mind about me," she went on, "you
go along and have your sail, while the
wind is so good."

"Perhaps Miss Burt could go to-morrow, and if so, Freddie may have another
sail," said Mrs. Davis.

"But to-morrow I'll be in New York
on business," said Jeremiah Storey, looking the disappointment he felt.

"Well, some other day, then," laughed
the woman softly. "I'll have Hugh
keep track of you and the weather and
Miss Burt shall have her sail, I promise."

"Thank you," said Molly, "I shall look
forward to it. Now you ought to start
before there is a change, and this brisk

sailing wind goes down. How well Freddie looks," added the girl, pinching the child's cheek.

"Yes, he has been very well, indeed, I'm happy to say."

The woman arose and Mr. Storey reluctantly followed.

"I'm coming back early," he whispered, as they reached the door. "I'm awfully sorry you are not coming."

"I'm sorry too," whispered Molly.

When they were gone the girl bounded into the kitchen. There was a little pang of disappointment to be sure, but still he was coming back. She found Bess shining up the faucets. "I'm going to make them so bright that Mrs. Julep can't help seeing them the minute she opens the door," declared Bess, rubbing vigorously. "I'm going to make them gold."

"Listen here a minute," said Molly, as she watched the frantic gestures of Bess trying to make the old faucets " gold."

"Yes, I'm listening."

"Bess, do — er — men like to eat things?"

"Eat things. What things?" cried Bess, pausing in sheer astonishment.

"Oh, do they like biscuits, and things."

"Of course they do, they like biscuits, an' meat, an' cake, an' corned beef, an' cabbage, an' everything."

"Well, we could not have corned beef and cabbage, you know, but couldn't we have some nice hot biscuit for him?"

"For whom?" asked Bess, in amazement.

"For Mr. Storey. He said he was coming back early, and I'm quite sure he'll be here to supper, and don't you think we ought to make some biscuit?"

"Just hot biscuit and tea won't be enough for him," said Bess.

"Of course it wouldn't be enough," repeated Molly, radiantly, "but we'll have a green salad, and quince preserves, Mrs. Julep's preserves are delicious, and cake, how does that suit you?"

"That would be very nice," said Bess, "there's no cake in the house, you know."

"But you can make some, Bess, can't you?"

"Oh, yes, I would just love to."

"And I'll make the biscuit, and the salad," declared Molly.

"Well let me make the cake first," said Bess, putting the finishing touches to the shining faucets, "the biscuit can be made the last thing."

This arrangement was agreed upon. Bess put away the scouring utensils, and having washed her hands started in to make the cake.

"While you are doing that I'm going out on the front porch for a breath of air, before I put on my apron," said Molly, and suiting the action to the word she went out leaving Bess singing merrily over her task.   Molly took a book to read behind the honey-suckle vine and so interesting it was that twice Bess came to the door to tell her it was time to start on the biscuit, but each time Molly was so engrossed in her story that the child did not like to disturb her and at last went

back to the kitchen and made them herself. Molly read on until someone
touched her on the shoulder and looking
up she beheld Bess very fresh and sweet
in a white dress with her best blue ribbons
in her hair.

"Now listen, 'mother,' and I'll tell
you all I have done, while you have been
reading. I have made the cake and the
biscuit, the children have been washed and
brushed up and are waiting for their supper. Now everything is ready except the
salad."

"Oh, I'll make that at once," said
Molly, rising, but just at that moment
there was a step. Mr. Storey appeared
at the little gate, and Bess hurried away to
wait on the children.

"Sit right down here. I must go in
and make a salad for tea," said Molly,
suddenly filled with the cares of house-
keeping.

"Never mind the salad, Molly, I want
to talk with you," said the man, dropping

into the seat and drawing the girl gently
down beside him.

"But there is not a thing in the house
unless I make up a salad."

"Who is it said something about 'a
crust of bread, and thou, beside me in the
wilderness. O wilderness were Paradise.'
I've forgotten."

"I didn't think *you* could forget
Omar," said the girl, a queer little smile
at the corners of her mouth.

He was silent a moment, then a sudden flush of comprehension swept over
him.

"Why it was Omar, sure enough, who
made us formally acquainted."

"Informally I am afraid it would be
called," laughed the girl.

"Ah! Molly, you thought I had forgotten, but indeed I have not. I remember it all as if it happened yesterday.
Davis and I had been hunting in the
wood at South Bridge and were hurrying
to catch a train when I picked up a pair

of gloves," " and a little book," added the girl softly; "and a little book," he went on with a laugh, "and Davis hurried on at a tremendous pace to get that train for he and his wife were dining out that night, but I lingered because I caught a glimpse of the girl, who lost the gloves."

" And the little book," she said again, reminding him.

" And the little book which proved to be a well-worn copy of the Rubiyat."

" And we met right at a giant oak that had been struck by lightning the year before and lay across our path," said the girl, taking up the thread of his narrative.

" And you asked me if I found anything, Molly?"

" Yes, yes," she laughed joyously, " and you were so long a time fishing in your pockets that at last you said, ' you'd better sit down if you want to hear what I've found.'

" I was secretly pleased at that, Jerry."

"And we did sit, and how we did talk, Molly! I remember every word, you said."

She threw out her hands with a laughing gesture of denial.

"I didn't know Omar very well in those days," he went on, "but before we parted, the best thing in his book was mine forever."

"What was that?" she asked quickly.

> "'*When time lets slip a little perfect hour,*
> *Oh, take it, for it will not come again.'*"

The girl smiled at him appreciatively, but Bess was at the door urging them to come in, and Molly remembering the salad flew into the little kitchen to prepare it. The color rose high in Molly's cheeks as she finished her task and called them in to tea. All went well until Mr. Storey took some of the salad. Molly, who at that moment had been studying

the face of her guest saw a look of min-
gled surprise and amusement as he
tasted it. He did not eat any more of
it, but Bess, with a growing girl's appetite had taken a generous mouthful and
made a little moué with her red lips.

"Oh, Molly, what is the matter with
that salad, it's awful, isn't it, Mr. Storey,"
blurted Bess.

Molly blushed furiously and took the
merest taste.

"There is something wrong with it,"
said Molly.

"It's the oil," declared Bess, "where
did you get the oil for it, Molly?"

"Right there in the closet," said Molly.
"Oh, dear, I wonder if I took the wrong
bottle."

"You certainly did," said Bess, going to the closet, and holding up the
half-used bottle labelled "machine oil."

The man laughed joyously and during
the rest of the meal Bess carried on an
endless amount of significant bantering

over Molly's efforts in the house-keeping line.

Shortly after tea Mrs. Julep arrived home from her trip to Chelsea. She was brimming over with the chatter of her visit, and in the evening they all sat on the little vine-covered porch until Mr. Storey took his leave.

"I wish she had stayed at Bella's a few hours longer," said the man in an undertone when the girl he loved had walked with him to the gate. "Thank the fates, Mollie, that Mint Julep isn't a lawyer."

"Why?" asked the girl with a ripple of laughter.

"Because no case she had anything to do with would ever be finished. She would never get through talking."

"She is the dearest soul in the world," said the girl, "and I won't hear one word against her."

"Molly," said the man suddenly, his voice earnest with a deep purpose, "I'm going away to-morrow and shall be gone the rest of the week. I wanted to say so much to you to-day," he went on. "Mollie, we love each other. We were made for each other and I want you dear, every day that I live. ˙

"I need your love, your faith, your helpfulness. When will you come Mollie? Can you not marry me at once?"

"Oh, not at once. Aunt Lida would never consent to that I know."

"I will see her just as soon as I come back Mollie. In the meantime I shall write."

"Mollie you need a wrap out there," called Mint Julep from the porch.

"Thank you, Mrs. Julep, I'm coming in at once."

"I think I had better go now," said the girl. "It is growing late."

"I must not keep you, dear," he whispered, and raising her little hand that rested lightly on the gate, pressed it to his lips and was gone.

CHAPTER XXXVIII

"AUTUMN NODDING O'ER THE YELLOW
PLAIN"

"THE summer is over at last,
Bess," said Mint one morning
many weeks after the events of
the last chapter.

The children were just leaving the little cottage for school and Mint stood at
the door watching them. "Yes," said
Bess. "the honeysuckle vine looks thin
and this very morning there was a thin
coating of ice in a pan of water that was
left in the yard over night."

"Well we can't expect summer all the
time. We had a good time out doors and
now it's time to do a little more indoors,"
said Mint; "run along now for school so
as to be nice and early, keep an eye on

339

Mamie, and Jimmie you look out for Bud."

When the little gate had shut behind them, Mint turned and entered the house and went into her sitting room.

She walked to the mantelpiece where a large white envelope rested against the black onyx clock, opened it and read for the third time since she had received it that morning the invitation engraved on its pages.

Mint Julep's face beamed as she put it back in the envelope. "So Molly Burt and Jeremiah Storey are going to be married and me and William are invited to the ceremony. Well I declare," said Mint. "I'll write this very day and tell William the good news and find out for sure if he's going to be home in time to go, for I wouldn't miss seeing Molly married for all th' world; and here I've been allus dyin' for a chanst to wear my purple silk and now it's come at last." And practical though she was, Mint Julep dropped into a chair while visions began to arise before her mind's eye of the splendor and glory of attending Molly Burt's wedding in a purple silk.

But alas Mint's day-dreaming was suddenly interrupted by a lusty shout from the twins and jumping to her feet Mint ran into the kitchen to find Ham and Egg on top of the kitchen table.

Ham had succeeded in reaching a bottle of glue on a little shelf, hence the shout of triumph. "I ish goin' shick tings wid dis," declared Ham.

"You air goin' to stick in the back yard and play or I'll stick things," replied Mint, and taking one under each arm she carried them out doors.

CHAPTER XXXIX

WEDDING-DAY FINERY

"I'M afraid we'll be a little late William, but I don't know as I'm feelin' bad ter cavort up the aisle at a weddin' in a purple silk an' a good lookin' man, though I think you got too much castor ile on your hair William; it's tricklin' down your ears — wipe it off an' when I take your arm jest let the other swing kinder graceful like, don't lay it crost your stummick, cause it looks then as if you hed a pain, an' you never did in your life, did yer?"

Araminta stopped long enough to look at her husband and screw her face into a smile.

"No I guess you don't know what a good pain is, men don't anyway and the Juleps are a healthy lot. I'm glad it's sech a lovely day, happy is the bride that

342

the sun shines on, 'though I don't take too much stock in that. There was Maria Stebins with a married life to her credit that 'ud make any ' grand sweet song ' seem like shoo fly 'sides a chorus of ten children, twins twict, an' all livin'.

" Well the day she married Jake Goodenough of Farnham, 'twas raining as if the flood gates of Heaven had opened and wuss than all, Jake slipped in a mud puddle goin' inter church and spiled his new lavender pants. The croakers was all shakin' their heads, but Jake jest stud up and shook his pants.

" No William the rain won't spile anybody's life 'less their willin'. Still I'm glad it's a bright day, there's no denyin', umbrellas at a weddin' ain't real inspirin'."

" Eh? Was yer goin' to speak, William?"

William who had been standing, hat in hand like a wooden image, on the threshold of his wife's boudoir trying to follow her varied movements, shook his head and rested on the other foot.

"I'll git my hat William and then I'll be ready — now jest wait 'till yer see a work of art."

Mint got on her knees and drew from under the bed a great bundle, opened it and held up for William's inspection, the largest hat in creation; it was completely covered with roses of various hues, while over all, rested two white doves, wings spread as if ready for flight.

The sight of this head-gear restored William's speech.

"Ain't it some heavy, Araminta?"

"Now if thet ain't jest like a man,— not how it looks, but if it feels comfortable. William Julep you'll never learn younger that style was made fust fer looks, if a speck of comfort was considered you're lucky; course it's heavy, but if 'twas a hod of coal I'd hev to stand it today. You an' me has been invited to a weddin' at the church. When thet sweet miss Molly sent me that invitation I vowed I'd go an' go in style an' I guess I've got a whole rose-bush on my hat,

'though I will say I never see purple roses
nor yet green ones but style can turn a
rose any color. I wrote to Bella Ball to
git me a hat; I told her I was willin' to pay
a good price fer something real stylish. I
said as how I'd go as high as three-ninety-
eight, but do you know she wrote ter me
that the price was appallin'— Appallin' is
the word says Bella, fer they wanted twen-
ty-five dollars fer a weddin' hat in one of
them stores thet had nothin' on it but a few
roses an' one little turtle dove.

" ' I could trim it myself as good ' says
Bella,—' go ahead ' says I, ' fill it with
roses an' put on two little turtle doves,' an'
she did, an' sent it an' I do think it looks
beautiful, though you'd be surprised William — one little turtle dove costs a lot of
money. But I admit I hev a weakness
fer some of the frivols of my sex. I like
flounces an' julery, an' I don't care who
knows thet my favorite perfume is
musk.

" Come along, William."

www.ingramcontent.com/pod-product-compliance
Lightning Source LLC
Chambersburg PA
CBHW032228010726

47494CB00002B/399